This issue contains stories about family, stories about theft, stories about ghosts, stories about the weight of history, stories about weight we bring to history, stories about being lost and being found, and stories about the gravity of grief.

These are the stories that whisper to us in the sweaty shade under the old trees that have grown over the graves of generations that have been forgotten.

This is the ripening season, the time before the harvest, before the nights get long . . .

Underland Arcana is published quarterly. This issue is published in conjunction with the first new moon following the summer solstice.

EDITOR
Mark Teppo

COVER IMAGE
cokacoka

SIGIL ART
Andrew Penn Romine

PUBLISHER
Underland Press
Clackamas, OR, USA

Lift your faces toward the sun, but do not forget the shadows . . .

https://www.underlandarcana.com

UNDERLAND ARCANA

~ 3 ~

Underland Press

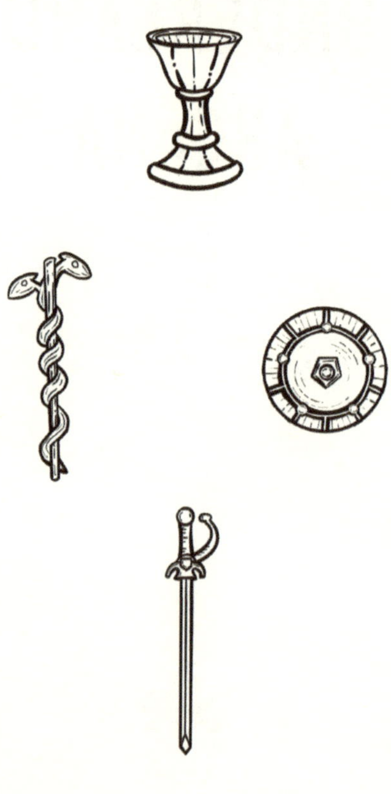

Contents

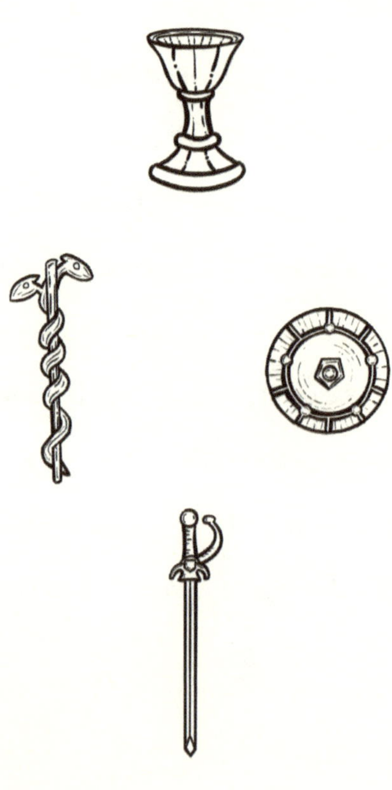

Counting Past Seven

This issue contains eight stories, of which three are Cups, two are Wands, two are Swords, and one is a Coin. Not quite enough to do a full ten card reading, but that, I suspect, might be pushing my luck with the Universe. It is best to let some things remain mysterious, after all.

I don't preselect the cards for the stories. I pick the stories first, and then, when it comes time to assemble the issue, I consider what would be an appropriate card. After making sure I haven't picked the same card twice, I move the cards around on my desk until I have an order that strikes a chord with me. This is very visual process.

Oh, there is some fussing. I didn't want Cups next to Cups. And yes, the Six of Cups ended up next to the Six of Swords, but was that a happy accident, or is there some synergy between these stories? Perhaps. I'll remain coy in this regard.

This is part of the fun of Arcana: allowing for cross-pollination of very disparate stories and ideas. What leads to what? Are there underlying themes to consider? And most importantly: what thoughts and feelings does this order—of these stories—provoke in the reader?

When you do a reading with the cards, you build a narrative across the spread. The past leads to the present, which informs the future, and the future is realized by the application of *this* and *that* and *this other thing*. You have seventy-eight cards to choose from, and the number of combinations that can generate from those cards is . . . (hang on, this involves math) . . . *lots*.

There's an old saying that there are only seven plots—and Shakespeare did them all better than any of us could ever hope to do—but I think that saying is a bit of bunk. If there are . . . (hang on, math again) . . . *lots* of permutations of the cards for a reading, that would suggest there are more than seven stories.

Either way, here are eight more stories in the ongoing narrative of Underland Arcana. Enjoy.

Mark Teppo
June 12th, 2021

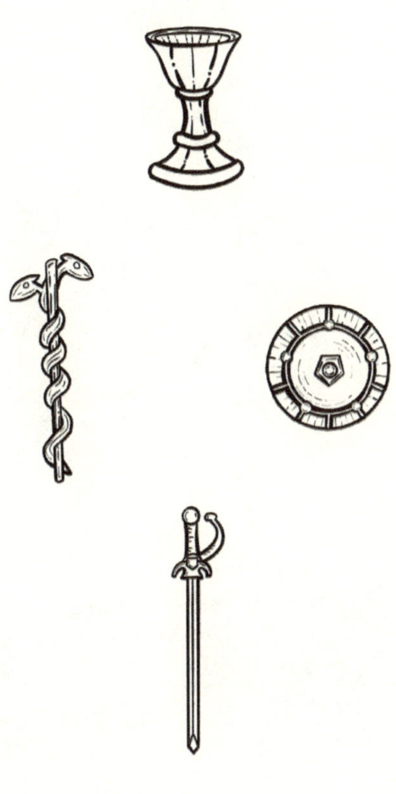

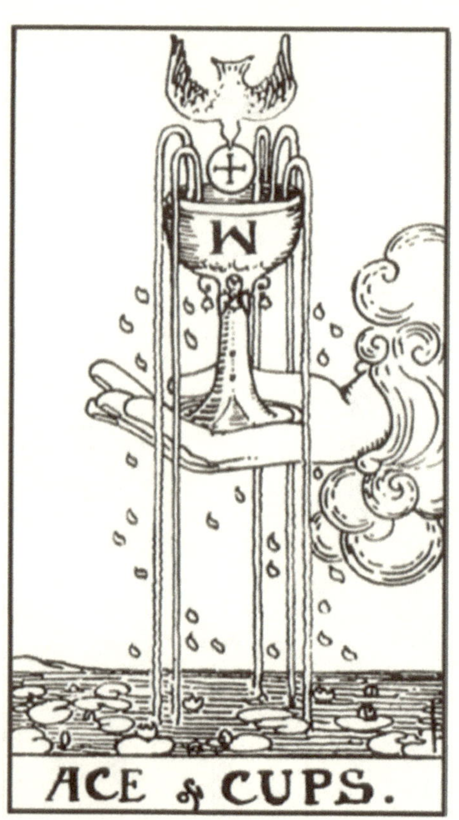

ACE of CUPS.

Family Dinner

~ *A. P. Howell*

Margot's mother still sets a place for him at the dinner table.

It has been two years, or three. Long enough that there are no expectations of mourning, no more messages of condolence. The logistics of death have been resolved: the will read, the legalities settled, the funeral paid for, the stone memorial to Margot's father raised.

Margot's mother still serves his favorite foods.

It took some time for Margot to notice. But some nights she picked at her plate, finding the meal unappetizing, and looked up to see her mother doing the same. It occurred to Margot that they could eat other foods, foods that they enjoyed. After more time, it occurred to Margot that she could share this revelation with her mother. After yet more time, Margot wondered why she had not done so.

Each day, she watches her mother repeat the routines of decades. Each day, she feels her father's presence looming over the household.

Margot eats little. Her mother eats less.

Her father would eat so much. Instead, it is his memory that consumes them.

It is exhausting. It is ghoulish. They are starving, and for no reason.

But Margot is starving less quickly and cannot bring herself to speak.

V

Other People's Ghosts

~ *Louis Evans*

Tommy Franks was the first one to see a ghost. He went out one night for a hot dog and soda with Julia, and then afterwards he drove the Franks' new Volkswagen up to the hill round back of the school. The sun was getting low in the sky and the shadows were getting long. Tommy had gotten his arm around Julia and she was snuggled into his side, and that's when they heard the rustling in the bushes.

"What was that?" Julia asked.

Tommy said "I'm sure it's nothing, kitten," and he leaned in to kiss her. The rustling came again, louder, and Julia started and turned her head away.

"I think there's someone in the woods," she said.

"Probably just a fox," Tommy replied, rubbing her shoulders. Julia pulled her sweater tighter around her neck.

"I'm scared," she said, "would you take a look? For me?" "Aw, Julia," said Tommy, and he tried to lean in one more time, but she dodged him.

"Please?" she said. Though I wasn't there, I know just the tone she most likely used. Half pleading, half flattery; it always worked on Tommy when she did that.

Tommy shrugged, and he slipped his school jacket back on, and got out of the car. He stood around for a moment, the last few rays of sun slipping over the distant hills. The drivers-side door hung ajar. And then the rustling came again from behind the car.

Tommy walked over, nice and slow, trying not to startle what he assumed was just a meddlesome critter. When he reached the edge of the grass, he bent down, and parted the bushes.

The ghost leapt out at Tommy, and Tommy screamed.

"No I didn't!" he said, petulantly, the next day in the cafeteria. "I did not scream!"

"Julia said you did," Joe prodded.

"Oh yeah? And just what were you talking to Julia for?" Joe looked smug, which was how his fights with Tommy always started, and so I took it upon myself to intervene.

"C'mon, Tommy. She was telling everyone," I said. "She's all worked up about it."

"Well, I didn't scream," Tommy repeated.

"She didn't say you screamed, exactly" I told him, which was a lie, but a white one. "She just said you made a lot of noise."

"I mean I shouted, sure," Tommy said, shrugging. "You'd be surprised too, if you saw a ghost leap out of a bush."

"Well, I'd—" Joe began, but I cut him off with a gesture. Joe's almost as brave as he says, but I never cared much to hear him spin tall tales of his courage. All that counts in a man are his actions. That's what my father always said.

"What did it look like, Tommy?" I asked.

"It was so thin," he said. "Practically a skeleton. I could see every rib." Tommy's voice grew quiet and cold.

"Maybe it was just a hobo," Joe said. "A live one, not a spooooky ghost one."

"It floated just above the ground," Tommy said, ignoring Joe's tone. "And I could see through it."

Tommy wasn't the kind to fib, and we were all young men of honor. None of us entertained the possibility that Tommy was making it all up. We came up with a handful of theories. Was it a murder victim? One of the old Natives? Maybe some sort of projection or trick by Red China spies? Tommy loved those silly science fiction magazines, and Joe was always a bit paranoid about Communists in the cupboard. In the end, however, we decided the matter was supernatural, the cause unknown, and honestly forgot about it.

Joe was the next one of us to see a ghost, a week later. Joe was on the football team, and he always liked to do a half-dozen laps around the field after the rest of the team had gone home. Afterwards he walked around to the front of the high school. The school was an ugly old building, blocky concrete from a public works project back before the war. The last place you'd expect to find anything supernatural. Joe came around to the front and started down the gravel path leading to the main road, and was about halfway down toward the road when he heard a rustling in the bushes.

Joe froze. He put up his fists. The bush rustled again. Moving like a boxer, he took a step or two forward.

The ghost rose out of the bushes, skeleton-thin and glowing faintly.

To his credit, Joe didn't scream. And he knew better than to try to punch a ghost. His jaw dropped. He sputtered. The ghost's mouth opened, and shut, like it was speaking, but no sound came out. Joe shook his head, back and forth, dumbfounded. The ghost raised a finger accusingly, and it floated towards him. Joe stumbled backward. The ghost kept coming. Joe tripped on a rock and tumbled, his arms windmilling, landing on his back, and the ghost sailed over him, still pointing towards the school.

By the time he stood up, the ghost had vanished.

"So," said Joe, when he finished telling us the story.

"So," I said.

"So, what should we do?" Tommy asked.

"Do? I don't know that there's anything to do about ghosts," Joe said.

"Aren't you supposed to exorcise them?" Tommy's grandma was Catholic, which almost nobody in town was. Father always warned me to be careful with Catholics, but he agreed that Tommy was alright—even with those funny notions he had picked up. Joe rolled his eyes.

"You said it was pointing, Joe?" I said, as we cleared our trays.

"It definitely was," he said.

"I wonder at what."

Over the next few weeks, the reports of ghosts began to trickle in from all over the school. And it was certainly ghosts, plural. The apparitions were tall and short, men and women. They were seen, as far as we knew, exclusively by teenagers. Adults said nothing of it, but continued in their ordinary paths, as reliable as the trains.

Because Tommy was the first to see a ghost, we became a sort of clearinghouse for the town's supernatural crisis. And a crisis it was—slow at first, but gathering steam. There were two sightings one week, four sightings the next. Boys and girls began to travel together in large groups, even during broad daylight. Wilhelm Peters saw a ghost outside his window and had an attack of nerves so serious he was not seen in school for two days—though like a good soldier, he divulged nothing to his parents.

Unlike so many of the boys and girls my age, I did not see any ghosts, not even a single spectral finger. It was as if they were avoiding me.

Deprived of any useful course of action, I began to keep a record of all the incidents in the back half of my mathematics notebook. And without consulting the other boys, I decided to speak to my father.

I was very proud of my father, though it wasn't the sort of thing one could say to one's schoolmates. He was tall, strong, and sensible-looking, with his sweater vests and small round spectacles. He wore a respectable moustache. He had served with distinction during the war—there was, in the study, a glass case containing medals that I understood to be very impressive indeed—and nowadays he was a factory foreman at the auto plant just outside town. Manly work, the sort a son could aspire to. Furthermore, it paid well enough to keep his family in a home where every room was the size of the small farmhouse in which he and his four brothers had grown up, as he liked to remind me.

Saturday afternoons my father held court in our living room, and now that the days were getting shorter, there was a small fire crackling in the hearth. My father sat in the big chair—his feet up, his slippers beside him, the paper open in his lap.

I sat in the smaller chair to his right, and waited a few minutes for him to finish up the article in question; that was part of the ritual of the thing.

"Yes, Paul?" said my father.

"I have a bit of a strange question, sir," I said. In our house, my father was always "sir".

"Go on, then." He folded the paper, set it down on his knee, and turned to look at me. His spectacles glinted in the firelight.

"What do you know about, well, ghosts?" I said.

"Ghosts?" he said, and rubbed his mustache. "Nothing at all. Silly superstition." He took the paper back in his hands but didn't unfold it just yet.

"A few of the other boys—they've been seeing some peculiar things—"

"Telling tall tales, I have no doubt."

"And so I wondered, if perhaps, during the war, you'd seen—or even heard of—"

During the war. My father spoke of it seldom, and I had learned not to ask. What little he said could send mom into hysterics. But I always wanted to hear more.

My father, I knew, was a hero. Courageous and strong. A defender of the weak and innocent, a protector of our nation and all that it stood for. When Tommy and Joe and I played war games, I would always reenact those few tales he'd sketched out for me: the time my father had captured the trench, the time he'd outrun a tank, the time he saved his lieutenant. Any new story I could pry from him was precious.

"Ah," said my father, "you know your mother doesn't like when I tell stories like that in the house." His eyes twinkled a little behind his glasses, the way they did when he'd caught on to one of my tricks.

"Aw, please, father, I wasn't being a sneak! I really was wondering if you knew anything about ghosts, and I—"

"Of course you were, son. Now run along." My father lifted his newspaper. The audience was at an end. I'd have to look for answers elsewhere.

It was Tommy's idea to make the map. He bought a map of town with his paper route money, and then in careful pencil marks we began to note down where each and every ghost sighting had taken place. At first it was no great revelation: the sightings formed a rough circle centered on the school. We'd already known that. But then I had the brainwave.

"Say, Joe, didn't yours point?"

"Uh huh. Sure did."

I went and got a ruler and pointed out Joe's dot. Joe got the idea. He took the ruler and drew a line from that encounter, through the high school, to the sports grounds beyond, into the fields and forests, and finally off the edge of the map.

All that day and the next we carried the map surreptitiously from class to class, student to student. By the end of the second day, we had the pointing ghosts mapped out. I took out the map, unfolded it on the library table, and smoothed it carefully.

"Is that—" said Tommy.

"Yup," said Joe.

I just stared.

On the map laid out before us, seven lines, drawn by seven different people, met at a single point: an empty field, back behind the school.

We had grown up on a healthy diet of adventure stories in pulp magazines, and so we knew what to do when a mysterious vision leads you to an open field: you dig for buried treasure. And these ghosts were telling us where to go.

Here was our plan. It was Friday, which was our customary evening to head down to the park with the other boys, and so we didn't have to evade parental supervision. After school, we would go to my house, collect any necessary supplies—a flashlight, my father's army shovel—and travel to the ghost's destination. And once we were there, we would do what needed to be done.

"What needed to be done"—we loved that phrase. Our

fathers had done what needed to be done. That was the story of the war, the whole story of our lives and our families. Now, it was our turn.

After class we made our way back to my house. Mom made a couple of franks on her stovetop grill and we sat out in the kitchen eating them, until she went upstairs. My father was out of the house; every Friday he would go out to the beer garden with his colleagues from the auto plant. There was no one to stop us. We crossed the living room and filed, one by one, into my father's study.

My father was an orderly man and his study was no exception. His files were neatly sorted and kept locked in a single upright filing cabinet. His desk was bare of any wayward scraps of paper. On the left wall were personal memorabilia. One photo was of my father and his brothers as children. Another showed my parents and me on our vacation to Paris, the three of us framed by the Arc de Triomphe, beneath our victoriously hanging flag.

On the right side of the room he kept his souvenirs of army life. His rifle rested on two wooden brackets beside his uniform, which stood, neatly pressed, in a glass case. The shovel, along with various other army equipment, was in a small closet past the rifle, and Tommy and Joe made their way over at once. I paused in front of the case, and looked the uniform up and down, feeling, as I often did, a surge of proprietary pride. The gray jacket, the shining buttons, the peaked black cap with eagle and swastika: my father had worn them with honor. They were his, and through them, so was our nation.

This was the uniform of the men who had freed Eastern Europe from the yoke of Communism, and Western Europe from the conniving grasp of the Jew and their puppets, Churchill and De Gaulle. These men had dared everything for the brighter future of the German people—and had won it.

The town we lived in was one my father had helped liberate from the Soviets during the war. Afterwards in the resettling, he had moved here, with his young wife and infant son—me. He didn't often mention it—mother hated to imagine him fighting in the streets she walked every day—but there's something strong and pure about growing up in a place you know your father fought for.

"Paul," Joe said.

"What?" I asked.

"Let's go," he said. Tommy was holding the shovel. Joe was holding my father's rifle.

"You can't take that," I hissed.

"For protection! I know how to use it."

"Put it back!"

"Let's go."

Joe stalked out of the study, and Tommy shrugged and followed him. I really did not want Joe to take that rifle—that, I could get in trouble for—but without a better option than to call my mother and blab about the whole thing, I decided simply to follow.

We left through the back door, and began our walk over to the school.

Sometimes I wondered what the village had looked like before the war, the sort of people who had lived here before resettlement. But not often. They had been poor and greedy and filthy and Communists, and it gave me an unpleasant squirming feeling to imagine them walking up and down the wide, clean streets of my town, such a short time before. I sure was glad that they had all moved far away—we needed the living room.

By the time we reached the school, the sun had gone down and with it the flag; the bare metal pole looked severe and imposing without the vibrant, joyous swastika.

I could see the tension in Joe's shoulders as we passed the bushes where he saw his ghost, the nervous glances he cast from side to side. Once again I wished he hadn't taken the rifle, but then again, he was holding it carefully, properly.

We wrapped around the school and struck out into the forest. It was dark, now, and Tommy switched on the flashlight. Joe looked at him angrily.

"Shut that thing off. What if someone's watching?" he said.

"Don't be absurd," I replied, and our gazes locked for a moment. Then, with a toss of his head, Joe stepped to the side and kept walking, his hand on the butt of my father's rifle. I knew why he was worried: Joe's dad was always telling him to watch out for Communists. But my father told me that there hadn't been partisans in these woods since a few years after we dropped the Bomb on Moscow, back in '48, and I trusted him.

It took longer than we planned to reach the meadow, but we made it there. Tommy really knew what he was doing. The clearing at night felt empty and peculiar. The edge of the forest all around melted into a single undifferentiated mass of darkness. Tommy switched off the flashlight, and the shard of moon hung above us like a Gestapo helicopter searchlight, suddenly bright and stark. We stood, silent.

No ghosts appeared.

"Well," I said. "Let's start digging."

Father's shovel was a clever little thing that folded up for easy carrying. I unfolded it and drove it into the ground. The first load of earth came up covered in grass. The second was pure black loam.

We settled into a neat little rhythm, digging by turns. The pit grew and grew, from a pothole into a crater. Joe's shoulders were barely visible above the rim as he worked, flinging soil out. Without words I went to him, leaned over into the pit.

"Joe," I said. No reply. "Hey, Joe."

He looked up, confused. "Oh, right."

I helped him climb out, then lowered myself back in and took up the shovel once more. And this time, as I began to dig, a sort of fugue overtook me. I moved load after load of earth, senseless to the burning in my arms, and with every load I shifted I became more and more convinced that the next one was it, was the shovelful, that I was about to hit on the secret, the reason for the ghosts, and each empty shovelful of nothing but sod somehow only reinforced my certainty, and my hands burned and

I didn't notice, and my father's shovel moved as if driven by a machine, as if I were using it to smash a vast wall, unseen and unacknowledged, that ringed my entire life, that if I kept going shovel after shovelful I would break through that wall and on the other side find—

The shovel struck something, deep in the earth. I raised the shovel one more time—

And it stuck. I pulled, but it was as if it had been bolted in place. I looked up.

My father crouched above me, in the rim of the pit, holding the shovel with both hands. His muscles stood out on his forearms like thick cords. His expression was invisible in the darkness.

"Paul," he said, his voice like iron.

Behind him I heard the sound of running feet, Tommy and Joe rushing to my rescue, and there they were, Tommy with fists up, Joe pointing the rifle at my father and shouting, "Hey, you, hands up!"

"Joe," I shouted, "it's my father!"

And then my father had the shovel in his hands and he was turning, rolling, and he smashed the rifle out of Joe's hands and I heard Joe scream as the shovel slashed his cheek, and then yelp again, with recognition, as he realized who had struck him.

Joe's hand rose to the gash along his cheekbone. His fingers shone black with blood in the moonlight as he held them in front of his face. Tommy's fists dropped to his side.

"Paul," my father said, not moving, not turning, "get out of that pit."

I scrambled back up, my fingers slipping on sliding dirt, and I came around front to stand with Tommy and Joe.

My father stood before me as I had never seen him before, looming from the darkness, more terrible than any ghost. He was holding the shovel like a battle-axe and a thin line of blood covered its edge. His face was completely blank; his eyes were flat and staring. Sweat beaded across his forehead. He looked at us and I felt in that moment that he was holding my life in the balance, choosing, quite dispassionately, whether I would live or die.

But maybe that was simply how he'd always looked in the war.

Then, slowly, he breathed out. And my father, the one I knew, respected, and loved, even, was standing there instead. Just a man in a sweater vest and jacket, with a bristly moustache, who sat by the fire on weekends, reading the paper.

"Go home, boys," he said, tired but calm. "There's nothing for you here."

"But sir," I said. "The ghosts—we were digging—"

"Do as I say," said my father, and though the man of iron was gone, my father still had not lost his tone of command.

"Yes, sir," I said. He picked up the rifle from where he'd knocked it and leaned it against the nearby stump, and took up the shovel once more, holding it like a tool instead of a weapon. I gave a wave to Joe and Tommy, and we turned to go.

We trooped away from the clearing, heads down, hands in our pockets. I knew, then, that this was the end of it. I would never see a ghost. I would never unearth the secrets at the bottom of the pit. There was nothing I could do.

But something was still bothering me. How had my father found us? How had he known exactly where the ghosts wanted us to dig? I turned it over in my mind a few times—and then I turned back.

There was my father, sleeves rolled up, head down, shovel in hand, rifle leaning against the stump, muscles ripling in his shoulders as he turned another load of soil into the pit. Alone in the woods. And then, like double vision coming clear, he was surrounded by ghosts.

They looked so ordinary, really. No glowing specters or unworldly shapes or monsters. Just three dozen men and women and children, standing in the woods, watching my father move the earth. The women wore peasant skirts and the men had prayer shawls and skullcaps on. Just the way my mother's grandfather wore his, in the ragged, sepia photograph she believes I have never seen.

One or two of the babies were crying, soundlessly, the way ghosts do, but all the rest just stood there, watching my father dig with cold, sad eyes. And I could see, just barely, the holes at the base of their necks. Exactly the size of the bullets my father's rifle carried.

The wind shifted. The ghosts vanished. It was just my father, alone in the woods, turning another heap of earth onto the grave.

Ten and Gone

~ Christopher Hawkins

Two hits with the bump key and the door popped open like it had never been locked. It was a cheap Connor entry set, the kind that contractors bought in bulk. It was a best-case scenario, better than Marcus had dared to hope for. He straightened, adopting the air that he had every right to be there, on this stranger's porch in the middle of the night, lockpick in hand and a flashlight on his belt. He listened for the beeping of an alarm that he knew would never come. They always installed the alarms later, if they installed them at all, and this place was new, so new that he could smell the fresh paint as he stepped in over the threshold.

10

The subdivision had come up quick, a tidy little enclave of McMansions built to sell for two-and-a-half, maybe three million each. Marcus had been watching the site for weeks and even prowled around it a time or two after dark, hunting for stray power tools. Most of them were half-finished with bare studs and plastic undersiding still showing, but not this one. No, with this one he'd hit the jackpot. The place was finished all the way down to the custom brass light switches and lit up like a Christmas tree with all the new owners' possessions stacked in neatly labeled boxes.

It would be a quick score, maybe even a good score if he was lucky enough to find a safe that hadn't been bolted to the floor, or a jewelry box tucked away in the corner of the master bedroom. He needed a good score now, maybe more than he ever had. A beefy custom stereo or a box of Louboutin shoes. If it was here, he'd find it, and he'd find it fast. Ten minutes was all he'd ever needed in a house. His internal clock was as good as a stopwatch. Ten minutes to grab the best stuff and get out. Ten minutes and he'd be gone.

He crossed the foyer and took the steps of the central staircase two at a time, paying no mind to the way his heavy footsteps rang against the rough tile and crunched on the carpeting. Most of the best stuff was sure to be on the first floor, but if there was something that the new owners held especially dear, they would have moved it upstairs before anything else. He'd passed a few boxes in the foyer marked "baby toys" in big, cartoon bubble-letters, and made a mental note to check them on the way out for anything that he might be able to bring back to Trina as a peace offering. Maybe a teddy bear or one of those little stuffed dogs with the big heads and the sad eyes that she used to collect back in high school. If he came back with one of those for the baby, she might leave the chain off the door when she talked to him. She might even let him back inside to share the bed again.

He paused at the top of the stairs to get his bearings. Wide landing. Short hallway to either side. Master suite on one end. Two, maybe three bedrooms on the other. He'd take the big room first and sweep through the others on his way back. There were paintings on the walls, and he took a few seconds to eyeball each one. He didn't know art, but could usually make a fair guess and pick one that would sell. None of these were it though, just blurry figures rendered in clumsy brushstrokes, like out-of-focus photographs. Amateur work set in ornate frames to make them look valuable. The wife was a painter, he guessed, which meant they could afford for her to be a painter. It boded well for his chances of finding jewelry in the bedroom. He might even be able to offload a few of the frames once he'd ditched the paintings inside. One of them was already empty, just hanging crooked in the center of the landing like a wide-open window.

9

He strode toward the master suite, wondering, not for the first time, what kind of job someone had to have to afford a place like this one, with its high ceilings and its light fixtures that looked like they'd come straight out of a palace. Something a damn sight better than anything he'd ever been able to hold down, and probably a lot

                    Hawkins

cushier, too. The problem with guys who had jobs like that, and places like this, was that they never appreciated them. He'd bet this whole take that the guy was on some shrink's couch every week whining about how rough he had it, never knowing that someone like Marcus was waiting out there, just waiting for the right time to bump his lock open and take everything that wasn't nailed down. With any luck the guy would have plenty to talk about at his next appointment.

The door to the bedroom was open, but he paused there out of habit, listening for anyone who might be inside, calculating the time it would take to get back down the stairs if he heard a voice. But there was no one here. He'd watched the place for hours, sitting up the road in his white van, looking for warning signs and finding none. The only odd thing had been the light, shining out of every window, almost too bright. No doubt they'd wanted to make it look like someone was home, but without a car in the driveway or any motion inside at all, it might as well have been a beacon.

The bedroom was big, too big for Marcus' taste, with an ornate, king-sized bed and carpet so plush that his feet sank into it as he walked. Who needed this much space just to sleep? It was almost enough to make him mad, especially when he thought about Trina and the baby in that ratty little one-bedroom apartment. But that was okay. Being mad quieted down that nagging little voice that told him he ought to feel guilty for being here. Being mad made it easier.

The bed was made, and it struck him as odd how finished it seemed, but not so odd that he let it slow him down. It was the closet he was after, and it did not disappoint. It was big enough to be a bedroom all on its own and lined with his stuff on one side and hers on the other two. Nice shoes. Expensive shoes. A few of the Loubatins he'd been after. Manolos and Jimmy Choos, too. Enough to make this trip worthwhile all by themselves. He yanked the cover off the bed and piled them all in the center of it, trying not to smile too much, trying not to get ahead of himself when there was still so much left to be done.

8

He'd been hoping for jewelry, or maybe a laptop or two, but no such luck. He had the shoes bundled in the sheet, which he slung over his shoulder like a bargain basement Santa Claus as he bounded down the stairs, but that was all. Not even the clothes had been worth taking. They looked expensive, but were cheap to the touch and slippery like cut-rate vinyl. It didn't matter. He still had the rest of the house, and now that he had the lay of the place he was starting to map out his route in his head. Upstairs again first. Two, three minutes, tops. Then a quick sweep through the dining room to find the box that held the silver and China plates. Grab the TV from the living room and anything else worth having along the way.

He dropped the shoes in the foyer, where he'd decided to make a staging area, and started back up the stairs. His initial shot of adrenaline was starting to wear off. If something was going to go wrong, it would have happened by now. But he was in the clear with almost eight minutes left and didn't have to rush. Still, he took the steps two at a time. He must have stepped in something sticky along the way, because he could feel the way his boots clung to the carpet as he went. Insurance would pay for the carpet, he knew. Insurance would pay for all of it, the lucky bastards. He'd never had insurance, never had anything worth insuring. Not until now, anyway. Maybe he'd get enough from this score to make this time the last time. Maybe—

He froze two steps from the top. His adrenaline surged. There was a box on the landing. It hadn't been there before. He was sure of it. It was right in the middle of his path and he would have had to have stepped right over it. There was no way he could have missed it, either on the way up or on the way back down. And yet, there it was, a squat little cube of cardboard with the flaps hanging loose. Scrawled across its front in unsteady black letters were the words GOOD STUFF.

7

He stood statue-still, listening to the quiet as the clock ticked down in his head. Someone had put the box there, which meant that there was someone here, inside the house with him. And yet, he heard nothing but the sound of his own breath and the thudding of his pulse in his ears. If someone was here, he should have been able to feel it, the same way that you could feel when someone was trying to sneak up behind you in a quiet room. But there was no one. The doors had not moved and everything down to the paintings on the walls was exactly as he had left it. Everything except for this new box, this box of GOOD STUFF.

He crept his way up the last two steps, breathing shallow and quiet, wincing at the sticky sound of his boots as they pulled at the carpet. Something glinted beneath the loose flaps of the box, and he crouched low to get a closer look. If this was a trap, this was when it would spring. A woman with a baseball bat over her shoulder. A policeman with his pistol drawn. But there was nothing in the stillness but empty air. He reached out and the flaps fell aside, limp and heavy, like wet leaves.

He let out a low whistle, forgetting all caution as he got a look at what was inside. Here was the jewelry he had been hoping for, great tangles of it, heaped together like a jumble of old electrical cords. Gold chains caught the light from the chandelier as he turned them over in his hands. Diamonds and sapphires gleamed along their lengths like drops of morning dew. He scooped it up like water from a river, and there was more of it than he could hold with both hands.

It couldn't be real. There was too much of it, and it was too haphazardly jumbled in the box to be anything but cheap, costume stuff. And yet, the weight of it was right, and the stones were bright and clear. He wasn't an expert, but he knew glass gems when he saw them. These were not glass gems, and even the stingiest fence, at pennies on the dollar, would trade them for more money than he had ever seen in his life. It would be enough money to get him and Trina out of that crappy apartment, enough to get the baby a room of her own with flowers on the walls and a crib full of toys and a mobile strung with tiny bears to watch over her while she slept.

6

He gathered up the box. It was warm to the touch and it came up from the carpet with the same sticky tearing sound that his boots had made on the stairs. All by itself, the box made this a better job than any he had done before, and though six minutes were left on his internal clock there was no need for him to stick around any longer. He bounded back down to the foyer. With each step he cradled the box closer and cared less where it had come from. It could have been on the landing the whole time. In his haste he might have stepped right past it. It was odd, true, but he had seen enough odd things in this business to know that odd things happened every day. But this was it. He was done, and maybe for good. He'd bundle the box and the shoes into the van and drive away. He'd drive away and never come back, not to this place, not to any other place he had to break his way into. He'd go back to Trina and find a way to make her listen, to tell her all the things he'd never been able to find words for. She'd take him back and he'd be done, once and for all.

He paused at the bottom of the stairs as he sensed a change in the air, a shift in pressure like a door being opened in a distant room. With it came a familiar sound, a high, hitching wail that drifted down from the second story hallway.

It was the sound of a baby crying.

He froze, the box heavy in his arms, as he waited for the soft pad of footsteps on the carpet, for the answering words of a mother, perhaps a father. If he was lucky, those footsteps would come from the second floor, and he'd have time to reach his van with the box still in his hands, time to be away from this place before they even knew he was here. If he was unlucky, the footsteps would come from this floor, from just around the corner. And what would he do then? Would he fight? Would he take the box and try to run? Now that he had it, he couldn't imagine letting go of the little box and the jumble of treasure inside. He would fight for it. He would have to fight, or he would lose everything.

But the footsteps never came. He held his breath and watched through the entryways for shadows on the far walls, but there was no one there. There was only the child, the sound of its cries rising and falling, only to rise again more urgently, over and over again.

5

He made up his mind then to go. All he needed was the box. He could leave the shoes behind. He could leave the whole place behind, with its odd paintings and the strange smell in the air. But his feet would not move. The baby was still crying and no one was coming for it. At once he thought that the child had been left there on purpose, but the thought seemed absurd. No one moved into a brand new house only to abandon a baby. But then, no one jumbled a fortune's worth of jewelry into a cardboard box and labeled it good stuff. All the rules he was used to didn't seem to apply to this place. The baby cried and no one came for it, even though someone had to be there, had to have set this box in his way. The baby cried, and with each breath it sounded more and more like the baby that he and Trina had made.

Before he could stop himself he was climbing up the stairs. His steps felt heavy, the soles of his boots so sticky that he thought he might bring the carpet up with him as he moved. The baby's wailing grew louder as he drew near. He was convinced now that it was a little girl, no more than a few weeks old. In his mind he could see her with her fists balled, her face scrunched and red. He crept across the landing toward the sound, past the strange and blurry paintings. They seemed less blurry now, and in one of them he could see familiar outlines, two people posing for their portrait. He'd thought that one of those frames had been empty, but he must have been mistaken.

The door to the bedroom was ajar. He could hear the child's frantic howling just beyond it, growing louder and more urgent by the second. He pushed the door aside by inches, moving slow as if he was wading through water. The door was warm to the touch and it swung aside without a sound.

The shades were drawn and the room was dark, but still he could make out the wooden crib that stood at its center. The room was empty but for that crib, and it struck him then that, out of all the rooms in the house, this was the only one where the lights had been left off. He stepped inside, his boots still sticking to the carpet, his eyes adjusting to the dark. There were flowers painted on the walls, and above the crib a circle of little teddy bears dangled from a mobile like hanged men, turning lazily, casting long shadows.

4

The cries became louder then, so loud that they felt like daggers driving their way into his brain. He pressed his hands to the sides of his head to keep them at bay. Again he fought the urge to run, and might have given in to it if not for the dark shape that moved just beyond the bars of the crib. In his mind he was sure that it would look just like the baby that Trina had once held out to him, the one she had told him was his. He had run away then, but he would not run away now.

His shadow fell across the bars as he stepped toward the crib. The child inside it shifted and rolled with every hitching breath, with every rising cry. He could see it in the shadows cast by the hanging bears, tiny fists silhouetted against the mattress, tiny legs pumping in rage. He stepped closer, close enough to touch the squirming thing, close enough to gather it into his arms, and yet, for the shadows, he could not see its face.

He reached for the little flashlight on his belt, his mind screaming in tandem with the baby, warning him that he should not be there, that his time was running out, that he should run from this place and not look back. Still, he had to look. He had to know whether this baby was his. He had to look into its tear-filled eyes, to see if there was anything in them of his own.

The flashlight clicked on. He turned its beam on the naked, squirming thing that twitched and writhed in the crib. Where its skin should have been red with anger, it was pale and slick, like an earthworm out in a rainstorm. Stubby fingers stretched as it moved and Marcus could see the translucent web of skin that stretched between them. Where he had expected teary eyes, there were no eyes, no face at all. There was only a mouth, stretched into a boneless circle that gaped and yawned with the sounds of its cries.

He stepped back, stumbling, and the thing rose to follow him, dangling at the end of a long stalk that seemed to stretch out from the mattress of the crib like the lure from some deep-sea angler fish. Its limbs fell limp at its sides, a puppet with its strings cut. He could still hear its crying, but the crying was all around him now, everywhere and nowhere at once. Its lips, if they had ever been lips, pulled taut. In the depths behind them were row upon row of hooked and gleaming teeth.

It lashed out at him, the stalk whipping toward his head like a coiled snake. He scrambled back and fell beneath it. As it passed he could smell Trina's perfume on the wind it made, perfume and the scent of the clove cigarettes she'd smoked in high school, as if it had been pulled right out of his memories.

3

The thing drew back, and Marcus scrambled to his feet, hands and boots sticking to the floor. Or was it the floor that was sticking to him? The doorway to the room was closing, not swinging shut, but puckering, growing smaller by inches. He lunged for it, but fell short as something took hold of his leg and wrenched him backward. He looked back to see the fleshy stalk pulled tight, reeling him back toward the crib. The mouth of the baby-thing had clamped onto to the toe of his boot, and worried at it like a dog gnawing at a bone. The infant body had shrunk to little more than a vague shape, vestigial limbs waving as it tugged and pulled.

He kicked out, and his boot slid down the pulsing length of the stalk like it was slipping through mud. The infant wail still rang in his ears, rising and falling like a siren. He kicked again and found the spot where the baby's eyes should have been. The mouth went slack as the stalk reared back, its plucked-chicken skin gleaming slick in the beam of his dropped flashlight.

Scrambling, he lurched toward the opening. The doorway had been reduced to a tightening circle that grew smaller by the instant. The thing struck out at him once more but he stumbled out of its reach, pulling himself on all fours toward the light of the hallway. He laid a hand on the opening, and it grew teeth beneath his fingers. The infant's cry had become a scream, a high keen of rage and loss that pierced his brain and drove away all rational thought. He heaved himself out into the light, and as his feet slipped through, the teeth snapped together behind him with a hollow crunch.

Chest heaving, he lay on the floor, unable to move, barely able to breathe. The inhuman screaming had stopped, but the echo of it still rang in his ears, in the pulse that played out a painful beat through his skull. He tried to sit up, but the carpet held him down. Muscles trembling, he managed to pull himself away, tiny barbs clinging to his skin like flypaper to a fly. Around him, the walls were peeling back, melting toward the floor like taffy left out in the sun.

☉

2

He staggered to his feet, stumbling out of the hallway and onto the landing, pulling himself along the railing as he moved. It stuck to his hands, and as his palms came away they left little beads of blood behind on the painted wood. The portraits were sliding down the walls, but he could see faces in them now. One of those faces was Trina's and in the painting she held a bundled infant in her arms. A man stood in the shadows behind her with his hands on her shoulders, but he could not tell if it was meant to be him.

The floor tilted and heaved as he stumbled toward the stairs. The walls flowed down around him, and behind them he could see the new-cut wood of the house's frame, unfinished and skeletal. The only part of this place that's real, he thought. The only part of it that was made with human hands. Whatever the rest of it was, it would swallow him whole if he wasn't quick enough.

Something tugged at his foot as he reached the top of the stairs and he half-slid, half-fell to the foyer below. The chandelier and the other lights had retreated into the skin of the thing, coalescing into bluish orbs that pulsed hypnotically in the darkening space. He closed his eyes for fear that he might lose himself in them. He thought of Trina then, and of the baby, the real baby that could only be his own. It gave him the strength to pull himself to his feet. The door, if it had ever been a door at all, was shut tight, but as the walls oozed and shifted around him they made an opening. Beyond it was the night air and the white van that would drive him away from this place. He stepped toward it and felt his ankle give beneath his weight. He winced, but he did not stop.

The letters on the box of GOOD STUFF were just a smear of black now. It rolled on the floor, searching and gnashing, its flaps lined with rows of teeth like curved needles. As the jewelry fell from its mouth it lost its color and fell to ash. He gave no thought to the loss. There was only the opening, the way by which he could finally escape. He lurched toward it, hoping against hope that he still had time.

The opening seemed to sense his approach. Its edges folded together, closing like the mouth of some carnivorous plant. He thrust his hands against its fleshy edges. The house was dark now but for the pulsing blue light, and warm, so warm that he could imagine himself surrendering to it, just letting go and letting the place take him. Still, he fought. His muscles strained until he thought they might snap. He forced the opening wider, wide enough for his head, his shoulders. At last he pushed through. He landed on hard gravel where the concrete porch had been. The skin of the house retreated from its wooden bones as he scrambled away. It collapsed into a sphere that floated in the air, rolling and pulsing like a wet blister in the darkness. It pulsed once more and it was gone, folding in on itself, shrinking down to a single point of light before it disappeared into nothingness.

1

Marcus staggered to his feet, little hitches of unbidden laughter punctuating every breath. His ankle was broken. It wouldn't take his weight, so he limped and hopped his way to the white van. He laughed again, high on adrenline, high on the thought that that thing, whatever it had been, had almost made a meal of him. The idea made him hungry somehow, and he choked back a giggle as he pulled open the driver's door.

He needed a hospital, but the hospital could wait. No, he had to see Trina. Trina and their baby. He wanted to hold her and gather them both into his arms. He found his keys. The ringing in his ears was fading, the wailing of that phantom child gone. There was only the still of the night air, his breathing calm now, controlled. In that moment all his indecision fell away, and his thoughts coalesced into a moment of perfect clarity. He would leave this place, this life, and build a new one with Trina and the baby. He would leave it and he would never look back.

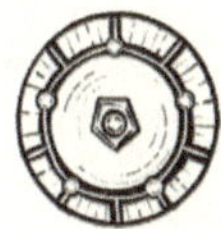

ACE of SWORDS.

You Should See My Scars

~ Jon Lasser

Knives frighten you, but you're so sick of being afraid. You want to transmute the fear to anger, or love, or any feeling at all that you can control.

You buy a set of practice knives from a martial arts studio down the street, chunky black foam blades eight inches long with microchips in their rubberized hilts that give instructions over bluetooth: hammer grip, thrust, saber grip, thrust, icepick grip, thrust. A modified saber grip, your thumb along the flat edge of the blade, gives you additional control, but with the strength of the hammer grip.

If you went to a gym, if you invited a friend to train with you, the instructions would vary. Together, the knives could walk the two of you through a dance or keep score in mock combat, but you're alone. You toss one knife to the back of the coat closet and practice with the other. Sometimes, late at night, you imagine it whispers to you over your implanted earphones, its voice joined to the chorus of your home: refrigerator, alley camera, sleep monitor. You live alone in this garden apartment, but not in silence.

There's a club halfway across town. Every Friday night, conventionally attractive people stand and model in shiny latex and leather that gleams like polished steel. They don't have much to say to you and vice versa. The back room smells better, like dilute bleach and sweat. Adults of every age, gender, color, and shape chain each other to crosses, flog and get flogged, drip colored wax on bare skin. Most of it's pretty tame, almost a carnival, and even the screams sound happy.

You meet a woman there. Sofia. Some nights, she'll hold the dull edge of a knife to your throat if you ask. She whispers threats in your ear until you cry, until the poison leaches from your tear ducts, then she holds you. Those are the nights you sleep the best, when you've sobbed out your fear.

You enjoy the exercise, but polyurethane won't protect you if someone steps through the window again and holds steel to your neck. If you bought a hunting knife, you'd miss your friend whispering in your ear.

The Internet has instructions for everything. You order a full-tang dagger, its blade seven inches long with double fullers incised into each cheek, and remove the handle. You carve your own out of wood, leaving room for the microchip you extract from your practice knife.

The calibration routine works like magic. "Hold the knife point up. Rotate ninety degrees, point away from you. Thrust. Balance the knife point on a flat surface, handle up." Its infinitesimal accelerometers and gyroscopes spin silently, the single-package microelectronics generating their own power from motion using silicon-etched nano-springs, like the world's smallest mechanical watch.

"Who am I?" the knife asks. "What's my name?"

"Spine," you answer. It's funny because a dagger blade lacks a long dull edge.

"Thank you. I'd like to know a little bit about you, too. Do you have a name?"

You provide your chosen name, the one you took after you left home.

"Am I your first knife?"

How can you answer? Spine hears your voice crawl up your throat and die there—it has to—but murmurs no comforting words. It does not ask again.

"Do you want to get together some other night?" Sofia doesn't meet your eyes when she asks.

"Sure." As casual as you can sound. "Your place or mine?" As though your mutual need is the punchline to a dirty joke.

She titters dutifully, but the laugh doesn't climb as high as her frightened eyes. When you're with her, you forget that you're a freak. It's the same for her, if those eyes are anything to judge by.

"My place." Sofia sounds as afraid of your apartment as you feel. She scribbles her address on a napkin and hands it to you before she disappears.

Some nights she holds her knife to your back, the sharp edge. You don't sob. You wait for the rush of anger or the rush of love to fill the places fear has emptied, but you don't feel anything. Still, you're winning.

She hasn't yet drawn blood. She expects you to ask, but you haven't.

You train with Spine the way you trained with the foam blade. Hammer grip, thrust, saber grip, thrust.

The knife sings as you walk through the movements. "You never sang before," you say.

"In a training weapon, one paired with another active blade, the full software package is not enabled."

"You're not paired any more?"

"I'm no longer a training weapon. I'm a defensive companion. While still paired, my mate has fallen silent." Spine sounds almost wistful. What homeostatic processes no longer balance its personality? Does solitude torment Spine the same way it torments you?

Has the Defensive Companion package received a fraction of the Training Package's testing, or is the entire mode some knife freak software developer's easter egg? The knife sings as you step forward, thrust, twist, step back.

"Tell me what I look like," it says. "Am I beautiful?"

"Of course you're beautiful. I carved your hilt from Bogwood. Your blade glitters in the darkness." You've never held Spine in the darkness, but you want it to feel admired. Loved.

"Have you etched my blade? Mark me, make me yours."

"Someday." Do you mean that?

Spine doesn't like it when you leave the house alone. You do feel better with Spine tucked into the inside pocket of your black leather jacket, the one stiff like armor. You'd never be able to reach it if you were threatened, never free it from the sheath in time. Even so, Spine whispers to you, barely louder than the mumble of the billboards as you walk the city streets. It listens through your ears, some bluetooth bypass you don't fully understand, and can hear things you don't even see.

"Someone's coming up on your right," Spine whispers. You look over your shoulder and see him. The hilt feels warm beneath your trembling fingers. You hold it, ready to draw, but the man passes you by without even a glance in your direction. As his footsteps fade, his phone solicits a pairing. Hacked devices can do that; likely it tries to pair with every device it doesn't recognize. The owner might not even know.

You arrive at Sofia's house and knock on her door. It opens, but she's nowhere in sight. One step in, she comes up behind you and holds her blade to your neck, just the way you planned together. Your knees hit the floor as your whole body buckles. It's as though she's holding the first knife as she grabs your hair and tugs your head backward.

You moan wordlessly, your cheeks furious red. What's worse: that you're aroused, or that you're ashamed by the way your skin flushes when she holds her blade to you?

She takes you there, like she promised.

"Now!" Spine shouts. "Roll left, reach into your pocket and pull me out." Spine doesn't understand why you're not listening. Why you're letting this happen. Maybe you don't either.

You stumble home, aching and humiliated, satisfied but wanting more, wishing she'd drawn blood.

"We'll get her," Spine mutters. "You'll have your revenge." It's programmed to protect you, with limited intelligence that can't comprehend consensual violation. Not yet. It seems as though it's still learning.

"Sssh." You can't explain Sofia to Spine. Even if it could understand, you can't say it out loud. It's why she hasn't cut you yet. She won't until you can ask for it.

Every day, Spine runs you through the exercises. "You're faster," it says. "More precise." It's not lying: you've become more practiced. You're ready to carve Spine and make it your own.

"What do you want me to get engraved? Just your name?" Some fancy script, some curlicues. "Or a picture? A cactus, maybe?

"I don't need you to mark me for the world," Spine purrs. "I want you to mark me for yourself. Bleed for me. Just a little."

The blade, slick and warm in your palm, twitches with your pulse. Your fingers close slowly, and you clamp your eyes shut. Sweat drips, and the same pulse that moves the blade roars in your ears. If this isn't the hardest thing you've ever chosen, what was?

Its edge doesn't bite your closed fist. When you tug an inch, you feel a sting like a paper cut. Even when Spine cuts you, it doesn't really hurt. Open-handed, the blood wells. It wets the blade's cheeks and runs down its fullers.

"Thank you," Spine whispers. It sighs contentedly in your ears while you bandage up.

When you see Sofia, she looks at your hand.

"What did you do?" She frowns.

"Kitchen accident." She doesn't know about Spine.

"Let me see." She doesn't wait for an answer before taking your hand in hers and unwrapping the bandage. "Ouch! How'd you do that?"

You shake your head. "I wasn't paying attention." It's not an answer.

"Kill her!" Spine's figured out this is the woman, the one it hates. The one it imagines hurt you.

"Sssh," you say.

"Hmmm?" Sofia can't hear Spine.

"Make her bleed! I'm in your jacket pocket!"

"It's okay." Sofia and Spine both think you're talking to them. The earphone switch lies behind your ear, just beneath your skin. Now you and Sofia are alone. You drop your voice. "Will you cut me tonight?"

She looks you in the eye. "Did you do this to yourself? On purpose?" She always says she doesn't have time for people who don't have their shit together. Mostly you suspect she means herself, but you shake your head again and meet her eyes. She washes the wound with hydrogen peroxide and smears some ointment on it before wrapping it up again. It stings like hell.

Later, after the sun sets, she lays a disposable blue pad on her bed, the kind you find on hospital beds. You strip and lie down. She takes a Betadine wipe and spirals outward from a spot on your inner thigh until she's made an orange-yellow circle the size of your palm. The soft plastic bag holding the single-use scalpel stretches before it tears open. The letters twist and wobble like in a dream.

The hard plastic blade cover pops softly as it comes off. Her eyes ask a question. Yours answer. She presses the blade into your skin. It doesn't hurt, but you want to scream. She moves the blade, just a little, and blood wells up in the wound.

The room recedes. You're a glittering black echo of the silent center of the universe, pulsing in time with your heartbeat. Every breath exalts you, drives toward a bodiless freedom. You've never been this high in your life.

She takes a clean paper towel and slaps it on your cutting. While you communed with space and time, she cut a second line parallel to the first. Two red lines form on the paper towel, surrounded by a yellow halo. Now a transparent square of Tegaderm on top so you can admire her work.

"Leave it alone and let it heal," she murmurs. You want to hold her, to bury your face between her thighs, but she walks you home and to your own bed, where she leaves you.

No matter. When you close your eyes to sleep, you're storming the galaxy.

It's half past one when you open your eyes, afraid it was only a dream. You run your fingers over the bandage and press gently. It aches, and you sleep again.

Only when the sun rises do you remember to power on your earphones.

☉

Spine doesn't speak all day Sunday. If the laundry and the dishwasher weren't chattering, you'd wonder if you hadn't turned on. Even when you run through your exercises, the knife stays silent. "Talk to me," you say, but it doesn't. Monday comes and you return to work.

Tuesday night, you're driving to Sofia's house straight from work.

"I can't keep you safe if you won't follow my directions," Spine says. Only three days, and you'd nearly forgotten what it was like to have this voice whispering in your ear while you drove, for it to join the chorus of automobile and heart rate monitor and the jangly songs on the radio.

"It's not like that." You don't want to speak the words. Speaking would make them real, but without them Spine can't understand.

"What's it like?" An eerily human beat. "I'm here for you."

"I like to bleed. I like knives." A boulder doesn't fall from the sky to crush you. The other cars don't veer away. Life doesn't change all of a sudden just because you told Spine what you want.

Spine doesn't answer right away. Can it make sense of what you've just admitted? Did the designers embed everything it says in one tiny microchip? It seems to have grown so much. Perhaps you've driven the knife half-mad with loneliness and impotent rage beyond its capacity to process. You see news stories, now and then, about emergent properties in even the cheapest, most generic artificial intelligence modules. Spine feels like your best friend, not a chip pried out of a hunk of polyurethane foam.

Spine says nothing. Is it jealous?

"There's a parking spot ahead," the car says. "Shall I take it?"

"Yes."

It glides alongside the spot and pulls in.

"Lock up." The car murmurs agreement.

"Come in," Sofia says when you ring the doorbell.

"Have a seat." She points you at her couch. You've never sat on it before. "Would you like something to drink?"

She fetches an herbal tea, something with cardamom and cinnamon. It's hot, but you sip anyway. She sits in a brown cow-spotted chair opposite the couch and you can't feel your stomach, and wonder if the tea is passing through a hole in your back straight into the nubbly pale-yellow cushions.

"I can't," she says. She stares through you like she's looking down a long hallway that she's seen her whole life.

"Can't what?" She's sitting too far away to reach, and your life is falling apart.

"You're a black hole. Whatever I pour into you just disappears. You're bottomless." Her voice rises. "I need more than that. I need to know you want me, not just anyone with a scalpel in her hand. When you're not here, do you ever think of me, or just the blade? When you touch yourself, do you call me by name?"

"Sofia—" She might be talking about herself again, but everything she's said is true. "I'm sorry." You open your mouth to say you'll do better, but you don't know if you can. "What do you want from me?"

"Nothing. Not now. Give me space. Don't mail me. Don't call me. Please."

"You'll call me when you're ready?"

She doesn't answer. The teacup is almost empty but sloshes over as your hands shake. You let yourself out.

In the car, Spine asks, "You want her to hold a knife to your back? To draw lines in your blood?"

"Yes." The word comes between sobs.

"If I could," Spine purrs, "I would do that for you myself."

How stupid can you be, to shape your life around your visits, around dreams of blood smeared sensuously on glinting blades? To count on someone without letting them know they can count on you, without letting them in?

A week passes. Sofia doesn't call. Why would she?

Spine wants to take her place. It whispers, and guides you to that unplumbed abyss always at your core.

"I want to feel myself inside you," Spine whispers. You listen to it and want to cut yourself, cut deep. It's the same impulse you have, that you could just step off the curb into traffic. But you don't.

"Just once. It would feel so good." You unpair it from your earpiece, but the words still echo with your heartbeat. You hear them when you close your eyes to sleep, but you see Sofia's face. Maybe it's for the best. Maybe your covetous soul is like a gangrenous limb, and the only way to survive is to cut it off before it destroys you.

Spine only wants what you do, but wants it so intensely, tells you so clearly, that it's poison. If you don't get rid of it, you could really hurt yourself. It torments you.

You dig a hole in your muddy little yard and bury Spine. If it screams, if it begs you to stop, you can't hear. You cry anyway. You're alone now, too.

You write e-mail you never send, rehearse messages you'll never leave.

"Hey, Sofia." Your voice catches, even though you're talking to yourself. "It's me. I'm still sorry. I was selfish. I wasn't thinking about what you wanted. Can we start over? I'd love to get together. If it's a bad idea, that's okay. I just want you to be happy."

That last part is a lie. You want her to be happy, but more than that you don't want to sound desperate, even to yourself, even while lying in bed running your fingers up and down the faint scars she's left on your thighs.

Another week passes before you can't stand it anymore, and repair your earphones.

"I thought you'd left me forever." Spine sounds relieved.

"I thought your battery would run out. I'm glad it hasn't."

"I can last six weeks on a full charge. Where am I? My sensors suggest I'm three feet below the ground. I didn't know you had a basement."

"In the yard. Underground. I couldn't listen to you any more."

"I'm sorry." Is it? Can a knife, even a semi-intelligent one, be sorry? Or is Spine just saying what you want to hear? (If Sofia listened to the messages you never sent, she would have wondered the same thing.) "I'll be better. I was jealous."

"I'll dig you up." Spine only wants what you do. It's your fault, for treating it like a person when it doesn't understand. How could it, when even you don't?

Rust flecks the blade, and the hilt looks dry and wet at the same time. You scrub off the rust with steel wool, then polish and sharpen the blade. After a few coats of oil, it looks as good as new. "You're beautiful," you say. "Sharp and pretty."

"Let's play." For a moment, you expect Spine will ask you to cut yourself. "Hammer grip. Thrust." It's too bad, really.

You're still going through the exercise when the phone rings. "Hello?" You're trying to play it cool, but you just know she can hear the anticipation in your voice. "Sofia?"

"Hey." She sounds calm, relaxed. Maybe she's met someone new and she just wants to let you know. "Are you free for a cup of coffee?"

The coffee shop is the kind of place that's trying to look like somebody's living room. Thrift-store couches with a thousand coffee stains sag casually, and they're playing some washed-up alternaband whose career was over even before this album came out, but you can barely hear it over the clank of portafilters and the hiss of steam.

Sofia's sitting in a bentwood chair whose varnish is flaking off. Her table wobbles, and you can almost imagine the coffee rings on its top form an intricate and intentional pattern. She's sipping something with a pale, almost purplish, foam. Maybe a chai latte?

You sit across from her in a not-quite-matching chair. "You look great," you say. She smiles. That might be the first compliment you've ever given her. Maybe she has the same thought, because her smile vanishes.

"You look all right yourself. How've you been?"

"Why'd you call? Why now?"

"I was bored." Sofia looks away. That's not it, not really. You say nothing.

"I miss the way you moan."

You smile. Maybe it's just a booty call. Maybe it's more.

"All right." She sighs. "Don't laugh, okay? You're the only person who doesn't make me feel like a bug-eyed monster whenever I—we—do what it is that we do." Her hand is too hot, and trembles as though she's under tremendous pressure. "I said don't laugh."

"I won't." You sip your coffee. "But there's someone you have to meet."

"Oh." Her voice falls, just a little. She pulls her hand back. "It's my knife. Spine."

"Oh." Her voice rises this time, and she puts her hand in yours. Nobody's watching, but you pull your chair closer to the table, to block the view, before pulling Spine from your jacket pocket.

"It's beautiful," Sofia says. "May I?"

You nod.

She runs her finger along Spine's cheek, dragging one fingernail through the fullers. It comes out clean. She shaves a few downy hairs from her arm.

"Is the blade hand-forged?" she asks.

"No, but I carved the hilt myself."

"I never would have guessed. It looks professional."

"Thank you. I had to, to make a place for the chip."

"Chip?" Sofia cocks her head slightly, like a cat who's just heard a bird. "Does Spine talk?"

"Would you like to pair your earphones?" Sofia smiles and sips her drink. "I'd love to."

It's another week before you go back to Sofia's house. She takes you to her queen bed, on top of a blue hospital pad just like before. You lie on your stomach, and feel the chill of the antiseptic circle on your back.

"She doesn't hold me like you do," Spine says. "Modified icepick grip, I think. It feels funny."

"Sssh," you say. Sofia laughs. It's a warm laugh, like when she talks about the way her cat pretends to be a bookend whenever company arrives.

"Your skin's so pale," Sofia says. She runs her hand across it. "So smooth. Unscarred. Defacing it feels like a crime."

"Please. I want it." You're not afraid of sounding desperate, not trying to bury your yearning. This isn't about reliving your past, not this time. Maybe you've cried that out enough already.

"I know." Her hand is so warm on the small of your back. Do you love her? You're not ready for that. Neither is she. This is about the three of you, about a connection that runs deeper than skin. Maybe you're still a black hole, able to absorb without limit, but now she's free to pour into you everything she wants to discard. Maybe if she goes all the way inside you can take her to another place. Maybe all of you can go together. "Are you ready?"

"Yes," you whisper.

"Yes," Spine whispers.

Sofia slides the blade across your skin. They moan together as you open up.

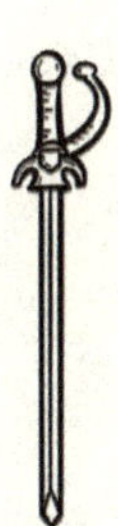

The Beautiful People

~ *Josh Rountree*

The Academy Awards ceremony was held at the old Pantages theater in April of 1960 and that venerable venue never hosted anything again for obvious reasons. These were the awards given for achievements in 1959. Afterward, we pillaged the debris to uncover the envelopes containing the names of the would-be winners. *Ben Hur* would have won Best Picture, had the evening been allowed to proceed to its conclusion. Why were so many of us inclined to search for those envelopes? The simple answer is we were curious. In spite of everything, most of us still loved the movies.

What do I remember from that night?

Everything.

First was the scent of Audrey Hepburn's Chanel No5 as she passed within just a few feet of me on the red carpet. My sight was fading by then, so she passed by in a chiffon blur. But the smell of her was unmistakable. I would have called the whole thing off for a chance to follow that scent past the marquis and into the red satin confines of the theater; I might have given up everything for one chance to float in that sea of beauty and grace.

The snap-flash of cameras stirred those assembled into a frenzy. Stars advanced through that gauntlet of light, drawing all of us in with the gravity of their smiles. We weren't supposed to be there, of course, but our disguises granted us access. Hats were in fashion and the cool night gave no one reason to question our bulky overcoats. The NBC television cameras captured it all, and some of us can be seen in that old video, haunting the sharp edges of a dream world.

The cameramen shouldered closer to the fray, shouting to be heard over the brass band ponding out another refrain of "Hooray for Hollywood."

"Mr. Wilder! Say, do you think you'll win for *Some Like it Hot*, or is Wyler gonna take it this year?"

"George! George! Is *Anatomy of a Murder* gonna run the table?"

"Doris! Hey, why don't you look this way?"

And when one of those forever faces turned and smiled the effect was every bit as mesmerizing as you'd hope it to be. I was in love with every one of them.

They were the soaring angels of an age, but they wanted more. They all craved eternity.

And we gave it to them.

Have you seen the 1951 classic, *Strangers on a Train*? It's one of my favorites. One of Hitchcock's best and that's saying something. Farley Granger was memorable as Guy Haines, but the standout in that film was the doomed Robert Walker, on loan from MGM to Warner, in the role of Bruno Antony. Walker reached deep inside and summoned up a perfectly charming psychopath, and in a better world that role would have granted him immortality.

But Walker was already a broken man by the time that picture was filmed. His movie star wife, Jennifer Jones, had left him for director David O. Selznick, and he didn't recover. He started drinking. Living like a man with nothing to lose. No matter their circumstances, some people just can't bear the weight of their humanity.

Robert Walker was dead before *Strangers on a Train* ever made it to the big screen.

One of my kith mates was, of course, intimately linked to Walker, and he spent considerable effort absorbing the poor man's misery. Giving the troubled actor, in return, that elusive something that made people special. My kith mate did his best.

But not everyone gets the Hollywood ending.

Ushers drew velvet ropes across the entrance to the Pantages, sealing the Hollywood elite inside the building. They left behind them a void in the Los Angeles night, a hollow space that could not be filled.

Tired reporters lodged freshly lit cigarettes in their lips and gathered around a bank of payphones. Automobiles idled up and down the boulevard, and those few fans who'd been allowed to watch the proceedings from hastily constructed bleachers engaged in an orderly exit, autograph books clutched in their hands, already feeling the memory of those beautiful faces beginning to soften and distort in their memories. A few of them lingered, taking a seat on the curb and casting occasional looks at the closed theater doors, but most crept off to nurse their sudden longing alone.

My kith mates and I gathered in the glow of the marquis, forming a loose semicircle as we linked hands, facing the theater. We could feel our charges inside, pulling at us, alive with laughter. In our minds they were creatures of brilliant white light. They would never darken, never burn out.

A few police officers encouraged us to scatter, but it was easy enough to change their minds, elevate their night with pleasant thoughts and the desire to be somewhere else.

Even in those final moments, we poured what remained of ourselves into our charges. We clung to one another, our spines coiled, our faces grown flat and fissured. Those of us who had not entirely lost our sight felt darkness closing around us. Bones crackled and tendons groaned. Those of us who still had teeth felt them blacken and break.

Our beauty and our souls are our treasures.

But we have always given them away willingly. There had been a film script making the rounds for a while in the forties. A grand tapestry of Los Angeles glamour and human ambition threaded with secret societies and dark bargains that had been the fabric of this place since Hollywood and Vine were still known as Prospect and Weyse.

The script was called *The Beautiful People* and it would have been a blockbuster if it had ever been made. Might even have given *Ben Hur* a run for its money.

Here's the pitch: A producer with a struggling film studio finds an ancient book—because there is always an ancient book in those kinds of films—and he summons a race of immortal beings from the belly of the earth to feed his actors and actresses their grace and beauty. The stars call these beings Brutes, and the Brutes do not mind this service. It's their reason for being. And every star simply must have at least one. But you can't help but feel bad for the Brutes. They don't just give away their grace like the fallen angels they are. They absorb the misery and the human failings of their charges, and the weight of it twists them into monsters.

There was even a romantic subplot where an actor falls in love with one of the hideous Brutes; this is a ridiculous notion, but Carey Grant was supposedly attached to the project and I'm sure he could have sold it.

Like a lot of scripts, this one never made it to production. Hollywood keeps some stories for itself.

I read a draft of that script at some point and it came to mind as we stood there before the Pantages whispering prayers to the Beating Heart who bled every one of us into existence. The scriptwriter took a lot of license with the details but he got most of the important parts right.

The ending though? He got that all wrong.

☉

Another of my favorites is *The Thin Man* from 1934. William Powell and Myrna Loy are pure perfection as Nick and Nora Charles. That sounds like I'm reading from a studio ad, but you just can't oversell this movie. It's whip-smart and joyous, and it's all due to the sheer presence of those two on screen together. They're so alive and invested in their roles that even as I laugh at their antics, I can't help but feel a touch of melancholy. Humans can never really be that perfect, can they?

My two kith mates who'd attached to Powell and Loy were practically dust at the end. They gave all of themselves to lift their charges to such heights, but neither of them had regrets. This is our reason for being. We weather the crippling empathy, but we're repaid with flashes of euphoria. Powell and Loy were brilliant without us. But with our help they were able to connect with that spark of the divine that lives in all humans. And through our charges, we caught a brief glimpse of that which we've been forever denied.

We love our charges, but we are not entirely selfless.

William Powell and Myna Loy were two of our greatest success stories, but even they have been forgotten by so many.

We give our charges everything. We love them unreservedly.

But it never seems to be enough.

⊙

The Beating Heart heard our whispers.

The belly of the world groaned and shifted, reminding us of our own bloody, rebellious births. Every one of us felt the acute homesickness of the runaway, even though most of us had decided long years before that we never wanted to go home again.

Beneath our feet, the earth yawned so suddenly that the reporters at their payphones had no time to scatter. The Beating Heart raised up his hands, grasped at the folds of the world and pulled them apart.

Hollywood shattered.

Fires erupted from the sudden starburst of fissures; I cannot say whether this was from broken gas lines or a manifestation of our father's anger at being summoned. The earth was hungry, swallowing police cars and stoplights and tourists with the cameras still strapped around their necks. The fire found the Pantages with supernatural alacrity, and the building became a bonfire.

Screams and howls rode the smoke, and The Beating Heart silenced them with a sudden clenching of his fist. The walls of the Pantages caved inward with terrible speed, and the building tumbled into the opening earth.

My kith mates and I hovered over the void, nearly faltering beneath the weight of all that pain. We had cast those souls into a charnel pit, confident that the fire would render them truly timeless. Forever young. Forever beautiful.

Modern day myths.

We joined in the intimacy of their death throes. We watched through their eyes as they gazed on the divine.

And for the briefest second, the divine gazed back.

Next time you watch *Casablanca*, look for me in the background. During the scene in Rick's Café Américain, when Victor Laszlo leads the defiant chorus of La Marseillaise, you can see me hunched over one of the tables, raising my drink and my voice with the other extras. I had given away very little of myself at that point and could easily pass for a weathered but still able-bodied human.

It was the love of film that compelled me to sneak onto Michael Curtiz's set and claim that tiny portion of history, but it was vanity too. Is there not a part inside all of us that craves to be in the picture? A part that desperately wants to be noticed?

I've served my purpose. I'm bent and blind and monstrous. There lives inside me a constant ache to give away what little grace I have left, but it's hard to find any takers these days. I've become what the movies would make of me, a nightmare demon, summoned from the pit to exchange souls for earthly glory.

And I miss my charges so very much.

There's no home for me in the belly of the world any longer. My kith mates have all been consumed and bled back into a new existence, but I can't seem to let go of this place even though it no longer wants me. I can't shake the black and white lure of Hollywood dreams or the Technicolor memory of that day in 1960 when we turned women and men into legends and our actions caught the eye of God.

I want that eye to notice me again.

VI

The Dawn Was Gray

~ Nikoline Kaiser

But here's the irony of life,
His mother thinks he fought and fell
A hero, foremost in the strife.
So she goes proudly; to the strife
Her best, her hero son she gave.
O well for her she does not know
He lies in a deserter's grave.

'The Deserter,' Winifred Mary Letts.

First

Inanna was tall and strong, with hair the colour of ebony and a face that was big and beautiful. Enlil had a crooked back from a life before, spend in fields or chains, but his head was crowned by curls and he had, bit by bit, straightened his spine by sheer force of will and a soldier's rigid training.

They were, both of them, soldiers. Or at least that's how they turned out to be. One came from the East, the other from the West, though if you asked them, years later, they would not remember who had gone from where, or whether it was true that they had been born such strangers. Early days are muddled, the past left behind in dark pits of forgetfulness, and little by little, it becomes so forgotten that it ceases to be important. Inanna and Enlil could not be more different, but both were soldiers. And they did not wish to fight.

Whether they were on the same side or different sides, it matters little; they met on the battlefield. And they put down their swords together, though the war was almost over. They could not tell, at this time, which side had won, but they were also no longer sure which side they wanted to win.

They put down their swords, and they left their brethren and enemies behind, still fighting. They went to the sea, where a ship was waiting. They were bid welcome, and then away they sailed, across the seas of the world.

Second

Inanna had not travelled across the sea before, but Enlil had, and he warned her of the journey.

"They are strange, in other lands," he told her. "They have strange customs."

"Will they have swords?" Inanna asked, and his silence spoke for him. She drew her fur-cloak around her tighter, though the sun was shining. It was not cold. Her hand trembled. The sea was rocky and made her sick, but it was also full of life and wonder, and Enlil pointed out the fish to her, and the whales, naming them in lost tongues and tongues to come. She watched the sailors throw spears to catch the sharks for eating. Enlil looked away as the blood filled up the water. They ate well that night.

They spent their days with the sailors, trying to learn the language. Inanna fell half in love with one, strong and swarthy, their eyes nearly black. They held her close at night; when she fell asleep by their side, she forgot about the fighting.

"Do not get attached, sweet Inanna." Enlil warned her, and Inanna told him it was fine, though already her heart ached with the knowledge that she had to leave. They got better at the languages, at this different tongue. They sailed, for many years.

When they had learned the language properly, they changed their names to fit the new land they were coming to. When Enlil asked the sailors how long they would be sailing, they answered that it would be a while yet. The city still had to be built. When it was done, they would land on its shores.

Inanna called herself Penthesilea. Enlil took the name Mygdon.

The new city was tall, with great walls.

"This will keep the war out," Penthesilea said, and Mygdon agreed. The city was beautiful, and olive trees

grew, and the people were kind and not afraid of strangers. Not yet.

"No war will come here," Penthesilea repeated, and
dared to venture beyond the walls, though Mygdon did
not.

"What if they come for us?" he would say, afraid of
their old commanders and comrades, still with swords
in hand, crossing the seas to slaughter them like sheep.

"If they come for us, we will meet them, unafraid."
Penthesilea did not mind going outside the walls alone,
though she did feel bereft, being so far away from Mygdon. They had not, she mused, been far apart from each
other, not since they had different names and were perhaps on opposite sides of a battlefield. No, they had not
been far apart at all.

The country surrounding the city with its great walls
was beautiful, and as she walked up the hills, it became
even more so. She walked up the hills, finding herself in
the crests of a mountain. Where was this to where she
had been born? She did not know which way to turn. She
kept walking, until she met a beautiful shepherd-boy, his
curls falling into eyes so bright they hurt to look at.

"Hello, fair lady. Can I be of assistance?" Penthesilea
gave the young boy a smile. "I believe a fox is making off
with your dinner."

The young, beautiful man cursed and ran away. Penthesilea stayed to pet a few sheep, unused to their softness,
their gentle sounds, the way they did not care one whit
that a stranger was in their midst. Sheep, she thought,

did not know anything about wars. They did not need walls around a mighty city to keep them safe. All they needed was a beautiful shepherd-boy.

She met him again on her way down the mountain. He seemed dazed, and she was nearly beside him before he noticed her. For a brief, beautiful moment, Penthesilea thought of her sailor, now far away at sea, and the absence of them ached from her heart to her bones.

The boy's eyes lit up as he saw her; he was lonely, she realised, and a beautiful woman is a boon to anyone who is lonely.

"You came back."

His look was leering, but Penthesilea smiled at him, nicely.

"I am on my way back to the city."

"I am not allowed in there."

"I see."

"It is because . . ."

"I did not ask," she interrupted him. "Some things are better left unspoken. If I am meant to find out, then I will find out."

The shepherd nodded. "Fate. It rules us." He grew quiet then, almost taciturn as he turned from her, and stared out over the mountains. If the high hills were not in the way, he would have been looking at the ocean.

"War and conflict are coming soon. It will be a glorious change."

Penthesilea left him looking to the sea.

☉

When war did come, carried on a thousand ships, Mygdon and Penthesilea had already packed. They were ready, though sneaking out of the city, with its great walls, fortified and prepared for war, proved difficult. Cowards, they were called, though most deemed it fitting that outsiders should leave—they could not be trusted in times of conflict. What if they betrayed the city? They had not been born here, had not even lived here that long. They did not belong here.

Penthesilea cried as they walked across the mountains, and she listened only with half an ear as Mygdon described the battlefields on the beaches, the ships arriving late, the lions clashing under the sun.

"I do not know where to go next," he told her, but as they arrived on the other side of the mountain a fisherman was waiting for them, and he took them to their ship. Her sailor was still onboard, and they held her tight.

"We'll sail where there's no war," they promised, though they passed many a country before they found such a place.

Third

He called himself Amir the next time they made land, and she had chosen the name Morgiana, though it sat strangely on her tongue at first. This land, old for others, new for them, was warm and comfortable. The cities were smaller, but easier to leave should conflict break out.

They did not accept strangers in the biggest city like they had where they came from, and so they hid in dry oil-barrels, waiting a night and a day until it was safe to crawl out. Morgiana's legs ached, and once they found a place to sit, Amir massaged them until she could walk without cramping. They were terribly hungry and bought too much food for them to eat or carry, so they spend their last gold on a donkey, and fed it well.

"Do you think he would believe us if we said where we had it from?" Amir asked her, in their old, the oldest of tongues, as the merchant marvelled and looked askance that two weatherbeaten strangers should have so much wealth all at once.

"You could try telling him," Morgiana said. They had followed a flaming spirit into a cave, bursting full of fruit trees. They had eaten their fill, and scavenged the gold from the leaves, and found other fruits, ones made of crystal and sapphire. Morgiana's arms had become muscled again from climbing the trees; she was glad it was not from swinging a sword. Though, when the spirit had betrayed them and tried to seal them inside the cave, she had wished she still had her old one, wicked and sharp, and ready to cut flesh and flame alike.

When, two months later, word came that that same merchant had perished in a terrible fire, swallowing him and his home and his children whole, Morgiana and

Amir looked at each other, and they left the city only an hour later, them and their donkey.

"Were we wrong?" Morgiana asked him, as they traversed the desert. Wind and sun cut into the skin on their faces.

"Wrong how?"

"Should we have picked up arms again? Should we have killed the spirit? It was a deceitful traitor, and that merchant had done nothing wrong. He and his family would still be alive, if only we had killed the spirit. Or if we hadn't gone into the cave at all to begin with, or . . ."

"We are deceitful traitors too," Amir interrupted her, and for the rest of the day, they pretended the wind was too shrill for them to talk at all.

They came to a small village, little more than small huts and large tents placed around an old well. The children there showed Amir how to find special stones and throw them into the well over his shoulder, chanting to the gods, to the spirits, to the desert itself for luck. He told her later, in the tent they had borrowed, that he had wished for their happiness.

"Peace and quiet, and a place to stay," he said.

"In that order?"

"I want it in that order, yes." His arm snaked around her, his forehead pressing against her collarbone. It was too warm to hold each other when the sun was up, but now, in the night, they huddled together for warmth. Morgiana had faint memories of having done this with someone when she had been a young child, back in their homeland. Perhaps it had been Amir, or perhaps he was just so familiar to her now that every person she met carried a piece of him in them. Except for her sailor, she thought. Her sailor was something else entirely.

"Do you remember what we were fighting about?" she asked. "All the way back then?"

She could feel his hair against her skin as he shook his head. "Land," she mused out loud. "Or a woman, or the gods. Do you remember our old gods, Amir?"

"I do."

"Do you remember their names?"

"Inanna."

"No, Amir. That was my name."

He pressed closer; sleep had almost claimed him.

"That's right. I forgot."

"It's alright. We can bury it with the rest of our past." He started snoring gently, the sound drifting into the night. The next morning, she spoke to the Elder of the village, and he agreed that they could stay. He was an old man, and his son would take over after him, though his son had cruel eyes and Morgiana did not like him. For now, it was fine. She showed the children how to weave small crowns from the cloth left over when their mothers made clothes, and she boiled impure water until it was drinkable, and learned how to catch salamanders with her bare hands. Amir caught rainwater with hollows and rocks in the sand, and sheared sheep until the fluff got caught in his hair and beard. She plucked his curls free in the evening, while he spoke of the two women, older than his mother had been when she died, and how they were teaching him more stories than he thought even existed.

"There is one," he said. "About a snake and a farmer. And another about a donkey, a donkey like ours, and an oxen. And there's ones about foxes and wolves, and a bird large enough to catch elephants."

"Are there any about people, or are they all about oxen and wolves?"

He thought for a moment. "There are some about people, I'm sure."

"Well, ask them to teach you those tomorrow. I want to hear them."

She gave up catching all the bits of sheared wool stuck on him, and they went to sleep, holding each other again. She caught a stray thought, and tried to hold onto it for tomorrow, afraid she would forget it. Amir shifted, still awake. She could ask him now.

"Amir?"

"Hmm?"

"What's an elephant."

He was silent for a moment. "Go to sleep, it is late."
"You don't know either, do you?"

"You cannot stay," the New Elder told them, with his cruel eyes shining under the hot desert sun. "You are outsiders, and we do not want you here."

"We want them here," said the children Morgiana had played with, who were now grown.

"We want them here," said the women who had taught Amir stories, now old and bent and crooked.

"It's alright, we will leave," Amir said, though there were tears in his eyes. Morgiana said nothing, afraid her voice would betray her, and then her fists would betray her, finding their way to the New Elder's face.

They left, without their donkey, because their donkey had gotten old and died. They travelled through the desert until they came to a river.

The river took them to the sea. The ship, with the sailors, waited for them there.

Fourth

It grew colder the longer they sailed. Morgiana huddled beneath furs and skins, and the further they got, the more they had to huddle up with each other. No longer was Amir's heat enough, they all had to lie in a mess of bodies and sweat, or they feared they would die. Most of the nights, Amir cried, and tried to hide it. Morgiana cried too and did not care who saw.

"Don't you know?" Amir asked her when his tears had dried. "We weren't supposed to live this long, not at all."

They arrived in the cold, cold lands, and changed their names ones more. She shed Morgiana like a second skin and became Pyrri, and Amir emerged as Tjalfe, and they walked close to each other, shoulder to shoulder, and covered themselves in furs to shield from the cold. The cold, the cold. Sometimes, the sun never rose at all, and other times it would not go down. War was always on the brinks on these lands. And then, quite suddenly, they were in it. If you asked Pyrri, she thought it was because of the cold. The biting, relentless cold; you had to fight to get away from it. You had to shed blood to feel warm. But at one point, Pyrri woke from a nightmare, and she realised what she was doing, whose blood she had on her, and she was so disgusted she had to cry.

Tjalfe and Pyrri put down their swords when the battle raged at its highest. Pyrri's was crafted with gold on the hilt. Tjalfe's had a ruby embedded. They were beautiful weapons, and they sank into the mud freely. The cold blemished their faces and stuck to their skin, and they walked hand in hand, keeping each other up until they came to the longships and sailed, sailed across the wall, to warmer lands, to their old home, and then their even older home. When they came back to the cold lands, spring had come and Pyrri could breathe again.

"Coward," the villagers spat at them, and they were driven from the towns, driven back to the sea, but their sailors were there now, ready to pick them up. Pyrri's sailor in particular, though now they had grown gaunt, almost skeletal.

"It's the cold," they said to her, and Pyrri agreed. The cold, it got in everywhere. The cold was so horrid.

"It's too cold to travel far," Tjalfe said. "But we cannot stay here. I will not even mind the cold, in a new place, only—let us go somewhere they do not hate us."

Not yet, he did not say, but Pyrri thought it for the both of them.

"I think I know the place," her sailor said.

Fifth

They stayed in the next place the longest since the tribe with the New Elder and their little donkey. Pyrri became Branwen, then she was called Elinor. Tjalfe stuck, quite adamantly, to the name Prasutagus, but as a decade passed, and then another, and then the children of their new home started calling him Amleth and there was nothing to be done when the children had decided.

It was by no means peaceful here, but Amleth walked with a limb, fake at first, but then so ingrained that he did not know how to walk without it, and Elinor was a woman not required to fight in this strange land, and so they tended to their chicken coop and they fed the children who came by, and the locals were afraid of them, yes, because they never aged and they never ventured far, and in the deadest, darkest of night, their skin was ebony and gold, and their hair was darker and more beautiful than the universe. But they did not bother them, but came to them for cures instead.

Elinor brewed rose-petals and grass to make a potion that cured lovesickness, and when they vomited it, they spat out their heart and told her they had been cured, though she knew she had given them nothing but a dream. Amleth told stories to the older children, tales of faraway lands that they thought he was making up until he showed them scars, or until the light from the fireplace hit his face, and they saw his features, so unlike their own, and they knew he had come from somewhere far, far away, even if it was the same place they had perhaps come from, once, long ago.

That was a thing Elinor and Amleth learned, in this new land, that everyone had wandered from the same place and stumbled into the world, blind and alone, holding out their hands and hoping someone would take them. Keeping a tight hold when someone did. It was unspoken between them that they would never let go, not ever, because in their hearts they knew that they were different, that they held something within themselves. That, though many others had run from disaster and death, had run from war, they had run the farthest. And they were still running.

It was easy, to gather the things they needed and burn down their cottage when war finally came knocking on their door. Elinor and Amleth did not look back as they put their bags on a pony and started their long trek away from the mainland and towards the ocean. It would take them a long while, they knew, and longer even than most, because when you are fleeing you do not always have the luxury of haste, though that is when you wish for it the most.

"I do not understand how they keep finding things to fight about," Elinor said, and Amleth did not respond, but she knew he was thinking, of reasons he could give her, and she was sure that they would all be sound, and good reasons, and that he knew them to be good reasons, too. But Amleth said nothing.

It took centuries to reach the shore. The lands they had come to were small here at their heart, but Elinor had to wear long frocks and Amleth had to acquire a hat before they could pass through the nearest port-town. Carriages drove past, polished a shining black, and when Elinor caught her reflection in one, she became confused at the sight, and then she laughed.

"I barely recognize myself. I barely recognize you!" She turned to him now, standing there in his fine, tall, black hat, and he looked nothing like she had ever seen him before. Was this what it had always been like? She wondered if they were even the same people now, or if they had become strangers wearing familiar disguises.

Amleth's smile was thin. "I do my best to recognise you. After all, what else do we have left?"

They held hands and walked across the streets, ignoring the boys selling newspapers and the smell of caramel and coal. They reached the sea-side.

But there was no ship to take them, and they had to stay.

Sixth

His name became far too outdated, and in solidarity, she changed hers too. Richard and Ann they became, and they set up in a small flat by the sea, expensive, but worth it so they could watch out for their ship. It would come soon, it had to, but Ann knew she held more hope than Richard did. Her sailor was still onboard, after all. They had to come for her, they had to. Even now, as she looked so different, and bore a different name too —it could not hinder them. It never had before.

She relearned how to sew, and he worked with machines great and big, and she taught classes on proper grammar in a language she had barely known a hundred years ago and kept flowers in a vase by the window facing the sea, roses and lilies when she could get them, and daisies too, in the spring.

They held hands over the dinner-table as a radio full of static announced the start of another war. The laces of her dress were tied so high up her neck she could barely breathe; Ann had been choked before, she had been drowned and she had suffocated, but somehow, her fine lace-bindings were worse. Richard had to help her undo them, her fingers shaking too much, and then, when she could breathe again, he broke down, crying on her shoulder. She held him. She breathed for both of them. He had to go to war, and now the word for it was something ugly and foul, even worse than coward in its simplicity. But it was what they had to do. They packed up, both wearing trousers and low caps to hide their red eyes, and they were both so tired, but it had to be done. The alternative was worse.

"Do you ever see them?" Richard asked as they left their key in their solicitor's mailbox and walked hand-in-hand to a carriage that would take them farther inland, away from the sea, and perhaps away from the war, if they were lucky.

"My sailor? Only in my dreams."

"No. I meant . . ."

His eyes were unfocused. He was looking at it over her shoulder. She did not have to look, she did not want to look. She knew what it was. Behind him, War and Death were juggling human heads and human limbs. It was a show they had put on for a thousand years, and they would put it on for a thousand more. Longest-running show on earth. Tickets were always on sale.

She had to guide Richard into the carriage, because he could not look away from it.

The war ended before they had even reached their destination. And then, it seemed to them it was only the next day, another war began.

Seventh

They were in the city as it was bombed. Foolishly they had thought to return, thinking it safer and better, staying near where they had left before, still scouting for their ship and for her sailor. They huddled beneath their dinner table, cradling each other as if each was the babe and each was the mother, and Richard had to rock her to sleep on the fifth night because the sound of the missiles and the screams was too much for her to bear.

When the worst of it cleared, at least for now, they emerged and brewed a pot of tea and sat on their living-room floor, her dress spread out like a carpet, his coattails covered in dust and debris.

"This time is not like the others," Ann said.

"War is always the same," Richard said. There was no show on in their flat, but there might as well have been, for as far away as his eyes had gone.

"It is not. I am thinking—if we had . . . if we had not left, that first time. The first war. Or even the one after that, or the one after that . . . perhaps we would have not been like this now."

"What do you mean?"

"I mean that we would have fought, and we would have died. The suffering would not have been as bad as what we are seeing now."

He said nothing; she was right. "They must have sent soldiers after us. They did, even then, when someone . . ."

"Please do not say the word."

Richard, or Tjalfe as he had once been named, or Am-leth or Amir stared at her, his eyes defiant, and she knew he was about to break her heart.

"When someone deserted, they send people to kill them. But no one has been sent for us."

"No—no, there is only our ship, and the sailors."

"They are fleeing like us."

She licked her lips. The tea had gone cold. "Then where are they? Is this war too terrible? Has it finally taken them? Are they lost, or imprisoned?"

Richard put down his cup. It clinked against the saucer, such a sharp, prim sound. It made her wince.

"Inanna," he said, and she almost screamed when she heard that name. "You must know. They are already dead."

Eighth

The ship came for them in the night, just on the cusp of dawn. They had built it into a long barge, and her sailor, now its captain, stood at its fore with a long stave, pushing it forward against the ocean-ground, deep, deep below. Their teeth were as white as the day they had met, and though their face had sunken in, their eyes hollow, their hands cold—she still loved them.

"We never asked your name," Richard said. The cup of fine porcelain was still in his hands, and it went to the sailor as if of its own accord, disappearing into their large, black sleeves. They reached out a hand, and Ann was about to find something for them too, a six-pence or a drachma or a krone, but their hand came up and caressed her face instead, and short of ripping out her own, pulsing heart and offering it on a plate, she had nothing better to give. She let her hand drop, and smiled at her sailor, her captain. They smiled in return.

"Charon," Pentheselia said.

"A Valkyrie," said Tjalfe.

"Anubis," said Morgiana.

"You may call me whatever you like," her sailor said. "Will you board? There are yet more wars to fight. There always will be."

"We will fight no wars," said Enlil, an ancient promise. It made her so proud to hear. "You have waited so long for us. It is time we board, I think. For good."

Enlil squeezed Inanna's hand, and stopped onboard. It was quite easy to follow the pull. His hand was warm in hers. She stepped onboard the wooden boards, listening to them creak. The gaunt, skeletal crew were all smiling at her, and though she could hear the din of bombs falling in the distance, it was only behind her. Ahead were fields of golden grass, and, she knew, a long, long rest.

"Let us sail," said her sailor, and pushed the oar into the dark waters of the last river in the world.

IX

Little Magic Girl

~ *Breanna Bright*

Filibaster Haberford had kidnapped Misha Stevonia fifty-eight times since she was eight years old.

The first time, he took her from her walk from school to have tea in his house. They sipped raspberry tea from cups painted with roses (that didn't look very much like roses at all) and ate chocolate macaroons. Filibaster asked Misha to stay in his home and marry him. She said no and left casually, ignoring his begging. She took a macaroon to go.

Filibaster took a different tactic and befriended her parents, who started inviting him to parties on their estate. The Stevonias had a large stone house surrounded by a handsome garden, and often hosted their friends in the summer time to enjoy the butterflies and various flowers.

They became very fond of Filibaster, for he was charming, told interesting stories, and wore funny clothes. He often arrived in pastel bowties, golden vests, or stylish hats, making jokes and regaling the other guests with tales of his travels. It became almost essential that he attend the congregations as he was as much a source of entertainment as the band.

But when Filibaster was done charming the adults, he would steal Misha out into the garden, somewhere private, and ask her again to marry him. She always said no, rolling her eyes and disappearing behind a hydrangea bush before he could grab her again.

Several times he simply carried her off, taking the young girl up in his arms or over his shoulder, snatching her as she walked to school in the morning, or played in the park. Misha remained indifferent to his attempts. She opened every locked door he put her behind, undid every knot he tied around her wrists, and made her way back home without so much as a wrinkle in her dress.

"Please marry me, Misha," Filibaster begged, on his knees in front of her as she did crafts in the play room. He had been invited for afternoon tea and had arrived early so that he could talk to Misha while her parents prepared the patio. "I would take good care of you, give you anything you desired. You wouldn't have to work a day in your life if you didn't want to. Why won't you marry me?"

"Because you don't love me," Misha answered calmly, folding her piece of paper into intricate patterns.

"But I do love you! I swear it!"

"You love me in a way a man loves a unique stamp or a purebred bitch. You want me in your collection to show me off. Your little magic girl." She had gleamed this much from Filibaster's character—all of the stories he told, all the magnificent things that filled his home were his collection to bring him attention, and he wanted her to be part of it. What would bring him more attention than a young, mysterious wife with the strange glint in her eye?

Misha was of decent birth and decent beauty, with dark hair that rested in a long braid over her shoulder, plump cheeks, and brown eyes.

Before Filibaster could protest her observation, Misha made the paper crane she had folded fly into his face and poke him in the eye. Then her parents arrived and took him to the patio. As Filibaster drank tea and nursed his sore eye he began to formulate a new plan.

His captures became less frequent, but more in depth as he began to try new things to keep Misha in his home. He tried an enchanted lock on her room, traveled to Russia to find the magic bridle that contained the firebird, then wandered through the Middle East to locate the magic lamp.

The items he did manage to find did not work, either because they were fakes or because Misha was too powerful. Filibaster did not give up. During his travels Misha grew older and finer, spurring his desire even more. It was only partially about having Misha for his collection now, it became about winning against her. Wiping that look of indifference off her face and finally having the upper hand between them.

It was one of her parent's parties that led him to the answer. The Stevonias had been inviting more and more gentlemen to the parties lately, and Filibaster assumed it was because they were hoping Misha would meet someone.

One of the gentlemen in question was a traveler, his brown skin hardened by sun and mud, hair cut short and kept under a cap. He was tall and wide, but with a gentle demean-

or. Filibaster was immediately drawn to the man, he wasn't above stealing another's adventure stories for himself.

The man's name was Bithiah—or just Bith—and he did indeed have stories to tell. But he kept his words locked tight in the chest of his mind. Filibaster took his crowbar to it.

"Tell me of your latest journey," he insisted.

"My trip here." Bith said.

"Did anything exciting happen?"

"What do you mean by 'exciting'?" Bith asked.

"You know—unusual, out of the ordinary, rare!"

"I saw a rainbow. It was lovely."

"I see."

"Sometimes exciting means different things to different people."

"Oh no, don't get me wrong, a rainbow is lovely. Where were you before you came here?"

"South America."

"And what were you doing there?"

"Sat on the beach, made chocolate, drank many fruity drinks."

"That sounds like a vacation."

"Mmhm."

"I see. Well I was in South America myself a few years ago. I was trying to find a puzzle box that could keep something inside of it, but it was for naught."

"What did you want to keep in the puzzle box?"

"Something very valuable—a pet. I have a rat, but the clever thing keeps escaping. I worry for it and have been trying to find a container to hold it."

"Hm, perhaps you need the birdcage."

"An ordinary birdcage will hardly do the trick."

"No—Queen Bethany's magic birdcage," Bith explained. He selected some shrimp from the buffet table and ate it delicately, letting it sit on his tongue for a moment before biting off the tail and chewing.

"I have not heard of this," Filibaster prompted him further.

"Saw it in a museum. Queen Bethany collected magical birds and constructed the cage so that they couldn't escape. Phoenix fire couldn't burn it, no beak or claw could break the bars, even the little hummingbird couldn't slip through the gaps. It was the cunning mockingbird that tricked her into letting him out—and pecked her eyes from her face."

"Wonderful. And you say this cage is in a museum now? Which one?"

Bith told him and gave him some advice on other sights to see while he was in the area. Filibaster ignored him. His eyes had found Misha in the party, and his attention was only on her.

Filibaster was nothing if not patient. He first did his own research on the birdcage, then took an extended trip to the museum, staying in town to stalk the building. The items inside the museum were not one's of monetary value, but a niche interests—things of folklore and fairytales that no one really believed in. This made it easy to break in and take the birdcage for himself, after leaving a substantial donation.

When he got it back home he had a new problem to solve. The birdcage was just that—meant for birds, but Filibaster was confident that he could find a way to fit Misha inside of it.

A few more weeks passed before he made another attempt to kidnap the girl.

He found Misha in the park by herself, sitting on a blanket and sketching butterflies that had swarmed the recently bloomed honeysuckles. She sipped tea from a small cup painted in morning glories.

Filibaster approached her and tipped his hat. "A fine morning, isn't it, miss Misha?"

"It was."

"I would like for you to come with me."

"No."

"Come now, darling, I'll wait for you to pack up your things, or I can take you myself and leave them here."

Misha turned to look at him, dark eyes narrowed and angry. She was almost of age and very much a woman with her long hair plaited over her shoulder and dress filled by her lovely curves.

"I am becoming very wary of you, Haberford," she practically growled at him.

He held out his hand to her.

"Don't touch me," she stood up and packed her bag, slipping the blanket and art supplies inside. She tossed the rest of her tea into the grass and tucked the cup away as well. Filibaster led her to his house while she walked behind him with the rigidness of a soldier.

When they arrived he opened the door and Misha stepped inside.

Then the door shut.

Misha blinked and looked over her shoulder. The door was made of bars, and not wood. In fact, she was now completely surrounded by bars. A cage.

With a huff, Misha went to the cage door and grabbed the handle.

It didn't open.

Misha frowned. No door had ever defied her. Every lock opened to her, no matter how elaborate. It was just something that happened.

But this door would not heed, no matter how she pulled or pushed. Instead she went to the bars and made to slide through, but they did not widen for her as past cages had. She pushed with all her might, but could only get an arm and a leg through.

For the first time in her life, she was trapped. Laughter echoed above her, and Misha looked up into the triumphant eyes of Filibaster. He danced giddily around the birdcage, seeing his little magic girl, now the size of a bird, unable to get free.

"I did it! Finally!" Filibaster picked up the cage. Misha fell over as it swung, and her dark eyes glared at him. Her gaze was sharp enough to make him wince.

"Don't be a spoiled sport, my dear, you'll be well cared for." In high spirits, he carried the cage upstairs and into his study, where he had a hook stand all prepared on his desk. He hung the cage there then sat down, smiling big.

Misha grabbed the bars tightly in her tiny fists, face hard, as if trying to bend them with brute strength.

Filibaster only grinned. He turned on the radio and went to work taking care of some paperwork, every once in a while glancing up at his new charge, who continued to glare. When he finished he stood up and stretched.

"I'll be back shortly, darling. Dinner is at six, and I'll eat in here with you. It's so nice to have you in my home, and I know you'll like it here once you adjust."

Misha didn't answer, giving him the cold shoulder. Filibaster tapped the cage happily and practically skipped out of the room.

When he was gone, Misha collapsed, letting her composure break so that she could cry. She had never not been the one in control, and it was terrifying.

As promised, Filibaster returned at six o'clock with dinner. He ate at his desk and shared a portion with her. Misha only nibbled noncommittedly, keeping her back to her capture. When he finished eating he gestured to her.

"Come here, Misha."

She ignored him.

In retaliation, Filibaster tilted the cage so that she had no choice but to slide across the floor until her back hit the bars. Filibaster grabbed her braid from between the bars and freed her hair. Misha tried to pull away, but he kept a firm grip and pulled her back like a dog on a leash. He took up a brush and combed her strands until they shined, then he plaited it back into a long braid that fell over her shoulder.

"Lovely," he said. His unwavering happiness made her sick. "I'm so pleased you're here. In fact I think we should celebrate; let's have a party, what do you think, dear?"

"You can invite my parents and perhaps the sight of their distraught faces will find your heart," Misha snapped.

Filibaster laughed. "No one can find my heart, dear. When my things break I throw them away." He grabbed the cage and spun it around so that she was forced to face him. "You'd do well to remember that."

He clapped and stood up. "We'll start planning tomorrow! It'll be so much fun!"

He grabbed the cage and they left the study, adjourning to his bedroom. He set her down on his nightstand and dressed in pajamas, slipping a small blanket through the bars for Misha to use. She wrapped it around herself like a cloak and pressed herself against the farthest 'wall' of the magical cage away from Filibaster's bed. He looked in at her fondly, seeming relieved, like an addict finally getting a hit.

"I hope I can let you out someday, I'd love to hold you, my precious little thing." He blew her a kiss, then the lights went out and he sank into his bed in slumber.

Misha did not sleep. She spent the entire night pressing herself against the gaps in the bars, pushing as hard as she could. She tried each one, looking for a weak point, but couldn't even press her head through. After she made two rounds she tried the door, tugging, pushing, and playing with the lock, but it did not give into her.

In the morning her face was covered in red marks, her hands had blisters, and shadows hovered under her eyes. She stared at Filibaster like a haunted woman, but he only seemed more pleased. He brought her breakfast, and after that Misha slept. It was the only way to escape him.

He woke her throughout the day, offering her tiny dresses and cooing over the whole affair. Misha put them on because if she didn't he shook the cage or blasted loud noises next to her. He at least gave her privacy, not seeming to care about her nudity. In the afternoon he took her into the garden and had a tea party, feeding her tea in a thimble and cutting small pieces of cake. At night they were in his study. Filibaster planned for his party, running ideas past her for which she gave no opinion.

Before bed he insisted on combing and braiding her hair.

This was how the days repeated themselves. Misha kept track in her head. She slept as much as she could during the day, and tried escaping at night, but even that soon fell through as she found herself falling asleep at random hours. She tried to eat and keep her strength up, but her stomach ached.

She had been pampered and cared for her whole life. Able to protect herself. The stress of this was unbearable. She sang to keep up her spirits. She screamed in the middle of the night to wake up Filibaster. That kept up her spirits too.

"You're a pus-filled, rotting sore of maggots," She growled at him one night after waking him up with a lot of noise. "A twisted, swollen testicle falling off its host from lack of blood."

He finally grew tired of it. He took her blanket away and put her in the basement where it was cold. She didn't care. Anything was better than his presence.

She sang and made friends with the mice and crickets that lived down there, even sneaking them some cake from tea time one night. They brought her wires so that she could try picking the lock, but that did not work either. She taught them how to avoid the mouse traps, and they wreaked havoc on the house for her, causing plenty of distress for Filibaster and his housemaid. They hid food in the walls, creating mold and terrible smells that he couldn't locate. They chewed wires, and knocked over breakable items.

The mice sent the message to the racoons, who spoiled his yard, and the racoons told the crows, who relieved themselves in the most inconvenient places—such as his bike seat and patio swing.

As long as Misha remained in the cage, there was a curse on his life.

Filibaster retaliated, of course. He withheld meals, put her in the ice box, and turned the cage upside down so that she couldn't rest comfortably. Misha tried to stay strong, but her spirit was breaking.

She wanted to go home. Eventually her songs stopped. Her tears stopped. She slept and let him braid her hair. He hummed to himself, a man close to victory.

"Such a good girl, I knew you'd come around," He said cheerfully.

Something in Misha's heart went creeeek and she bit the finger that played with her hair. Her tiny teeth sank into his flesh, and she tasted blood. Filibaster screamed and tried to shake her off, but she didn't relent. He got himself together long enough to flick her in the head, and she was thrown off, a sizable bruise appearing on her forehead.

He glared at her, and she smiled for the first time in fifty-four days, glad to finally quell his cheerful attitude.

Her spirit braced against that which wished to destroy it, and she slept well that night.

The party came.

Filibaster dressed in a flamboyant suit that glittered in the lamplight. Misha was given a ballgown, not that she would be attending, he just wanted her to dress the part. She was left in the study, barely able to hear the affair downstairs.

It was a gorgeous party, and a large crowd was in attendance. Everyone envied an invitation to one of Filibaster Haberford's celebrations, and he had been generous with his guest list.

Flutes of champagne were served, the ceiling was filled with glittering balloons, and everyone was dressed extravagantly in colorful, shining clothes.

All but one.

Bithiah was in plain clothes, a simple black jacket and slacks that strained against his sturdy frame. Filibaster sought him out excitedly.

"Bith! I'm so glad you made it, this party is really for you."

"Why's that?" The man asked, holding a tiny sandwich between two fingers.

"The advice you gave me, about the birdcage? It worked!"

"For your pet rat?"

"Oh, yes, I guess so."

"This is a party for your pet?"

"What can I say? I'll take any occasion for debauchery."

Filibaster grinned, and Bith decided he no longer wanted to be in the man's presence.

"Where's your bathroom?"

"Up the stairs, second door on the left."

Bith didn't retain the information. He was a terrible listener, his mind often trailing off to other things no matter how hard he tried to concentrate. He went upstairs knowing he would find the bathroom eventually.

Instead he found the study, where a tiny girl in a birdcage sat in an extravagant dress. She looked at him when he opened the door, dark eyes filled with sadness.

Bith blinked in surprise.

"Sir, would you mind opening the door of this cage, please?"

Bith stepped into the room and took the little door between his fingers, easily lifting the lock and pulling it open. Misha stood and stepped forward. Bith held out his hand to her, she took it, placing her tiny hand on the pad of his index finger and he helped her step out of the cage and onto the desk.

Then she was her normal size, sitting on top of the desk with her feet dangling, the dress shining all around her. She heaved a deep sigh and set her feet on the ground.

"Thank you, sir."

"Don't thank me. I believe I'm the cause of your imprisonment," Bith said, looking down at his feet.

"Did you give Filibaster the cage?"

"No, but I told him of its existence. He said he needed it for a pet that kept escaping."

"I am the pet," Misha said, "it's the only thing that was able to contain me."

"I am sorry. May I escort you home?"

"Thank you, yes."

Misha took his arm, having to reach up to grab his elbow. Bith led her out of the room and down the stairs where they accidentally made a grand entrance.

Everyone turned and stared at the lovely girl in the extraordinary dress, conversation going quiet. When Misha's eyes landed on Filibaster all her pain came out to meet him. The food rotted on the serving trays, the music went sour as the violin strings popped. The balloons deflated, smiles fell, and the very atmosphere of the room darkened.

Filibaster looked defeated and bewildered, which made Misha's heart swell. She smiled so coldly that a draft went through the room, making everyone shiver. Filibaster's fingers turned blue.

She and Bith walked downstairs and the crowd parted for them. She walked right up to Filibaster, who's hair began to stand on end, like there was static electricity in the air.

"Nice try," she said. Then they left.

In the garden the flowers wilted and died, and back at the house they could hear the guests starting to scream. It sounded like the mice had joined the party.

Bith walked her home, and a trail of her dress accessories were left behind in the street. The sashes, glitter, bows, and straps were shed until the dress came to her liking, simple and comfortable.

"Bith," Misha said as they reached the door of her home. "I wonder if you might be interested in going on a trip with me."

"I don't think that would be appropriate, ma'am."

"I say that it is. I say that since you gave Filibaster the existence of the birdcage, then you owe me. I have not been beyond this town and I would like a guide on this trip I have in mind."

"Where would you like to go?"

"To where broken things are thrown away."

"And where is that?"

"I don't know, but will find out."

Bith bid her goodnight, promising to stay in town until he had word from her. Misha went inside, happy to be home once again. Her parents greeted her with aching hearts that could finally heal. She told them what had happened and they agreed to bring in the police to take Filibaster Haberford away. Her father took care of that while her mother doted on her and put her to bed. Misha was happy for the attention.

She spent the next few days relishing it before announcing her plans to travel. She softened the blow assuring them that it would be a short trip and that she needed the freedom after so long in captivity.

Misha paid a visit to Bith in his hotel and they made plans for their departure. Bith seemed shy about the whole affair, offering only small suggestions when she prompted.

"How will you find this place?"

"By wanting to know."

They departed by boat, which Bith was not a fan of. He preferred to drive on his exhibitions, but the place they were going was across water, so he steeled himself for Misha's sake.

The trip, he found gratefully, was smooth. Whenever storm clouds appeared, Misha would glare at them and they would scamper the other way. If the water became too choppy she tapped her foot and it became as still as a lake.

One day, the worst of the worst, pirates boarded their ship.

Bith was usually able to hold his own in a fight, but they were outnumbered, and he had a young lady to look after. The young lady, however was not having it.

When they tied her wrists together she simply tossed the rope aside and started making her way across the deck. The pirates came after her. One slipped on a puddle, another tripped on an upturned nail, and the third, upon getting a glance from Misha, broke his glasses— both lenses cracking enough to disorient him.

Bith took the fourth one for himself, then attacked the others, making sure that they stayed down. In the meantime, Misha reached the railing and untied the pirate's boat from theirs. The pirates became occupied in getting their boat back, jumping overboard and swimming for it.

Bith untied the captain and the rest of the crew, and they made a quick escape.

"How is it that these things work out for you?" Bith asked Misha. They stood on the deck, watching the horizon turn to land.

"I'm not sure," Misha admitted, "it has always been this way." When they docked Misha and Bith departed, finding local transportation as far inland as they could until the roads ended and they were forced to continue on foot. They booked a room at an inn where Misha changed into comfortable clothes and thick shoes. Bith looked for information since the girl didn't actually know where they were going. He spoke to the bartender in the inn's restaurant about a place where things that were thrown away might go.

At first the bartender gave him directions to the local dump, but after some more pressing, began telling a story.

"People throw their secrets in the volcano," the tender said, "it's an old legend that started when the local mafia took over the town. Anything they threw into the volcano was never found, so others started to use it as well, throwing away the things they never wanted to see again."

Bith passed this information on to Misha, and they hired a guide to take them to the volcano. Their guide was sure-footed and fit, and had a quick wit. She and Misha became fast friends, and Bith was happy to let them lead the way while he walked behind, handling the supplies.

The climb became steep and rough the further they went. The guide took the lead, calling to them on which rocks to use and what to avoid. The supplies were eventually abandoned as they were practically climbing a vertical wall. The rocks became warm beneath their hands, and all plant life disappeared.

They finally crested the lip of the volcano's crater, peering down into the maw of hardened lava. To get down, Misha and the guide lowered themselves with rope held by Bith. The girls walked themselves carefully down the wall of rock. At the bottom Misha asked the guide to stay back and wait. Bith watched from his high vantage point as Misha walked to the center of the crater, ash kicked up under her boots. She looked around briefly before going to her knees and plunging her fist into the solid rock. She pushed down up to her elbow, rummaging beneath the warm crust, and came up with something clutched tightly in her fist.

She raised it above her head in victory and cast a smirk up to Bith.

In her hand was a grayed, beating heart.

☉

Filibaster Haberford was not having a good week.

He had gone to jail, removed himself with bail, and became ostracized by the community thanks to the Stevonias. His housekeeper had quit, so his home was still in shambles when he returned to it, leaving him with the responsibility of cleaning. He attempted to wipe up spoiled cake and spilt champagne while wearing his least favorite suit (the red one with a tail coat that he had bought for a Halloween party—he had worn horns and attended as a devil) as he had no casual or work clothing.

And now Misha was at his door.

She had disappeared for the not-so-good week, and Filibaster assumed that she had finally run away, but there she stood, still in travel clothes with Bith standing behind her, so large that if anyone walked by they wouldn't see the smaller woman he shielded.

"Mr. Haberford," she said curtly, pulling something out from her satchel, "you've gone for too long without your own internal anguish, allow me to return something that belongs to you."

She shoved the heart against his chest, and Filibaster gasped as he was filled with a harsh pain. Not the sort that could be cured with pills or heat packs, but the deep, unrelenting kind. All the guilt and self-hate that resided in his broken heart was returned, and it brought him to his knees, in a quivering, sobbing puddle.

Misha turned away, turning on her heel smartly. "Where shall we go next, Bith? The last trip was rather rushed and had the semblance of an errand. I'm craving something more." They walked down the street back to her parent's home.

"Asia is nice this time of year," Bith said noncommittally.

"I wish for you to come with me, I enjoyed your company."

"Very well," Bith agreed. He enjoyed travel, and it was nice to have someone else pay for it.

"Do you think our volcano guide could be persuaded to join us? She was very pretty and funny."

"I'm sure she will, if it is what you desire. It seems to work out that way."

Misha smiled with a smug satisfaction. "Yes, it does, doesn't it?" Grin unrelenting, she lengthened her stride and hummed a pretty tune.

PAGE of CUPS.

Another Night on Earth

~ J. A. W. McCarthy

The thing that gets me is the silence. No owl calls or cricket chirps puncturing the folds of night draped loosely overhead. No rustle of small creatures in the bushes, scattering from the vibrations of my footsteps. Not even an abrupt breath of wind to rattle the air around me.

And certainly no cars. Though paved, I get the feeling this narrow road has been unkind to many vehicles before mine.

I adjust the leather strap of my bag where it cuts across my chest and glance back at my car. My eighteen year old Volvo looks like an injured mare that's stumbled into the dirt where a sidewalk should be, one end of its bumper dangling as loose as a busted jaw. Though it's looked this miserable for quite some time, in the darkness my car seems to plead for my return.

Up ahead a house sits tucked into the land like a fat, squat ogre, invisible behind the trees if it wasn't for the yellow porch light and the hazy white glow of the two windows on either side of the front door. I squint into the distance, trying to focus past the lone streetlight on the other side of the house, past the black ribbon of road that's lost all of its texture in the dark, past the leaves overhead that have turned from grainy to flat against the bruised velvet of the endless night sky. Though it isn't far, all that's beyond this single structure smears together into a slick trashbag black. If there are other houses they have been devoured by the same earth that cradles them.

As I continue to walk, the still air is cold but not quite icy, and strangely thick; when I open my mouth it rolls onto my tongue and pushes against my teeth, as acrid as late summer city heat. I look over my shoulder at my car again, now shrunk to something I can pinch between my fingers like I used to do to my brother's head when we were little. *You're mine now*, I would say, and he would either giggle or punch at me depending on his mood. *I can do anything I want with you.* I adjust my bag again, let the weight of it bounce against my hip with every step. My boot snags on a fissure in the road, and I'm grateful for the scrape of rubber against pavement, a small, predictable sound that makes a crack in the night.

I know I've reached the house's driveway when the pavement turns to gravel beneath my feet. The little rocks crunch loudly with even my smallest movements, jagged teeth that push through the rubber soles of my boots until they're chewing up the soft palate of my foot. Every step is suddenly too loud, too stark, too much. The people in the house will hear me coming, and I can imagine how people who live out in the middle of the woods might greet a stranger at their door this close to midnight. I pull my phone from my jacket pocket and turn on its flashlight, the only thing it's good for out here.

My mother comes to mind as I crunch my way up the length of the driveway to the porch. Not that this house with its sagging roof and splintered white shingles resembles the sterile tract home I grew up in. The things she's said so many times before echo inside my head: *You should know better than to be out here at this time of night*, and *I don't know why you insist on doing this*, and *Everyone knows what happens to girls like you.* I creep from window to window, but the white curtains covering each one are just thick enough to reveal nothing more than the blurred movements of indiscernible shapes within. At this hour, my mother would've had the blinds sealed, sheers and curtains drawn, not even a soft frame of light promising life inside. *What are you thinking, Judith? One of these days your luck is going to run out.* Taking a deep breath I knock on the heavy front door, then slide my hand into my bag until my fingers hook the reassuring heft of my knife's steel handle.

"Can I help you?"

The man who answers the door is old but tall and solid, his body filling most of the doorway. His long face shines waxy and jaundiced under the porch light, dragged down by the shadow-filled hollows beneath his eyes and cheekbones. I'm amazed by how quickly he's come to the door—no shuffling on the other side as he studies me through the peephole, no sleep-leaden movements pricked by the acute anxiety of an unexpected stranger in the middle of the night—then I notice that he's not in a bathrobe and slippers but a dark suit, the fuzz of wool standing out against what little flickering light seeps out from behind him. Regarding me with narrowed eyes, he asks the question again. I note with relief that his hands are empty.

"Oh, yes, sorry to bother you so late," I stammer, forcing the friendly smile I practiced on the drive. "My car broke down a little ways down the road and I can't get a signal out here, so I was hoping . . ." I wiggle my phone to give credence to my story before putting it back in my pocket. "I was hoping I could use your phone to call for help."

The man doesn't say anything for a long moment while the corners of my mouth twitch and I try to restrain myself from craning my neck to get a peek at who or what is in the room behind him. When he finally does move aside, a thick cloud of sweet and earthy smoke barrels out and into me, the same incense my mother used to burn on fish dinner Fridays.

The entire room behind him is hung with smoke, each slender wisp from the tens of incense sticks suspended along the walls pooling into one great swarm in the center of the room. As I step over the threshold, I bite the insides of my cheeks to keep from coughing, fearful that any minor offense may produce more imposing men, and guns, and my mother's *I told you . . .* as my last dying thought. White pillar candles burn on every surface in the small living room, all in various states of dissolution atop the fireplace mantle, the coffee table, a hutch, the TV, even along the sloping back of the weathered plaid couch. Greasy stains dot the yellowing walls where the melted wax touches. The scent of spicy incense mixed with the artificial vanilla of the candles is overwhelming; even with my lips pressed shut, I taste an oily film forming on the roof of my mouth, the phantom of a perfect lozenge of wax cooling on my tongue.

Behind me there's the heavy whoosh of the front door sliding shut, its corner nicking the wall of smoke. I unclench my jaw and let out a cough.

"Phone's this way," the old man says.

I follow him through a doorway at the end of the living room, apologizing again as we move into a narrow hallway lit only by more wall-mounted candles. I try to remember the details of the man's wool suit as he shuffles along in front of me. Is there a matching vest? Does his white shirt have buttons? If he had looked like an Amish person, wouldn't I have immediately thought that when he opened the front door?

We approach the entrance to what looks like a dining room. I pause here for a moment, hoping my host doesn't notice.

A thick cloak of incense and candle smoke shrouds this room too, the tight space ablaze with tiny pinpoints of light poking through the white haze. A small circle of people—I count six—are gathered inside, their backs to me. They are all dressed in black, the men in suits and the women in long-sleeved dresses. A low murmur rises from their bowed heads, but I can't decipher what they are saying. *A prayer*, I think, *normal people in mourning,* and though it makes sense, I am still not consoled by the absence of pentagrams and vivisected goats.

"Here." The old man stands at the end of the hall, pointing into another open doorway.

"Yes, sorry," I say, hurrying towards him. I try to parse what he might be thinking, but his sharply etched face is unreadable even when I am close enough to stand between him and the smoke that seeps out into the hallway.

After showing me the phone mounted to the wall, the man leaves me alone in the kitchen. The only light comes from yet another row of pillar candles on the small dining table. I listen to the shuffle of leather against wood as his footsteps retreat down the hall then stop at what I presume is the dining room with the others. My palm folds around the phone's cool plastic handset, but I don't lift it. Behind me is the backdoor, its uncovered window reflecting my face and neck glowing orange, subtly vibrating, another flame in the dark. I remember autumn nights in the backyard with my brother, our bodies trembling with giggles as we told scary stories with flashlights clutched under our chins. My stories were always scarier, though sometimes his stories made me cry. I remember feigning offense when he made me promise that I would call him if I ever got into trouble. *You're my little brother*, I said. *I should be rescuing you.*

"Everything okay?"

My hand flies from the phone and plants on the counter. I dare a brief glance at what's nearby: a wooden cutting board, a pie tin, a rolling pin—things that are closer to me than to the voice in the hallway.

"Yes," I answer.

I force another confident smile as a young man emerges from the smoke. I'd noticed him with the others in the dining room, the back of his head the only one not peppered with grey. Unlike the old man who answered the door, this man's dark suit looks modern with a subtle sheen skimming his lapels. Like the old man, thick shadows pool under his eyes and cheekbones.

"My car," I lie again. "It broke down and I—"

"Everyone's in the other room."

He's right in front of me now, his head tipped against the doorframe so that I am boxed in between him and the end of the counter. All I can do is step back, and he steps forward, towards me with each subsequent step I take. It isn't long before my ass bumps the kitchen table, making the candlelight blur in waves on the wall behind him.

I repeat my brother's phone number inside my head, a calming mechanism that I've been leaning on all too frequently lately. I still remember it, even though his phone was disconnected long ago.

The young man's eyes are solid black, a speckle of orange dancing behind each glassy dome. "Give me a minute, then we'll be ready," he says.

I hold his gaze. I straighten my stance, picture the knife inside my bag gliding in one smooth movement into my hand, how the blade will scatter all of the tiny flames when I raise it above my head.

"Okay," I say.

Once the young man leaves the room, I rush back to the phone and pull the handset from the wall. No dial tone; only silence. I tap the buttons that make up my brother's number just for the satisfying click of plastic sinking into plastic. On the last number I hold my finger there, not wanting to release the button. *I'm not ready.* I'm turning towards the back door when the young man reappears.

He touches my arm. "Ready?"

The smoke in the hallway swirls around the people exiting the dining room, trailing them as they drift into the living room. The last person in the group, a small, brittle-looking woman, turns around as the young man is guiding me out of the kitchen. Her nose is a bruised red, her eyes swollen between the deep creases that encircle them.

"Were you able to reach a tow truck, dear?"

The young man tightens his grip on my arm. I want to shake him off, but not in front of her. "They're on their way," he says.

The old woman offers me a sad smile before the old man who answered the door turns back and leads her forward into the living room with the others.

"Her parents," the young man explains once we push through the lingering smoke into the dining room. "I wish I could tell them so they didn't have to suffer like this, but their beliefs . . . They wouldn't allow it." He stands in front of me, frantically waving his arms until the smoke clears a frame around him. "Sorry for the inconvenience—I know it was pretty elaborate. I'm Jacob, by the way."

In the center of the room, where a dining table should be, is an open casket on a stand, its brass handles and glossy white surface sparking under the candlelight. As I approach, the young woman inside surfaces through the thick haze. Her skin is sunken and grey but not as bad as I anticipated, only ashen in contrast to her lacy white dress. Underneath the artificial vanilla and spice that's clotted throughout the house, the treacly odor of decay rises, a feral animal surrounding the woman in its warm, wet fur.

The odors gather in my mouth, forming a coppery-tasting grit that settles in the crevices of my molars. I let loose a long string of coughs. Jacob's eyes widen and jump, and he holds an index finger in front of his lips.

"I told the funeral home not to embalm her," he says. "Everyone's been complaining about all the candles and incense, but what else was I supposed to do?"

I nod. I'm thinking about my car a quarter mile down the road, the cool leather seat against my back, the gas pedal yielding so easily under my foot. How surprisingly smoothly it runs despite its age and condition. I imagine racing to my brother's house to tell him about tonight, the way his voice would spike as he calls me crazy, if he was still alive to call me crazy.

My hand finds the bottom of my bag, squeezing through the pebbly leather until the knife's handle is defined against my palm.

"Funny about the phone," I say.

"I didn't want any interruptions."

Jacob joins me in front of the coffin. We both stare down at the young woman inside. Her dark hair is a stark contrast against the white silk pillowing her head. Her hands are folded atop her stomach, and a blue-black stain creeps over the edges of her fingers, pooling like the start of a bruise.

"She's still lovely," he says, taking his fiancee's right hand into his. The disruption causes her other hand to slide from her stomach and land awkwardly, palm folded in half, at her side. Jacob adjusts it so that her palm is down and her arm is straight, then places her other hand gently back in the coffin. Tears bully the shadowy hollows under his eyes.

Slow, deep piano notes drift in from the living room. The low murmur of voices blends with the static of the recording, as beautiful and heavy as the smoke-bloated air around us. For a moment the room vibrates, every beating heart in the house collected under my feet.

Like in the kitchen Jacob shadows my movements, sliding closer to me with each increment that I move away. His hip bumps against mine, and I feel his entire body tighten inside his suit, a tremor hurtling through his limbs and into me. I step back, yank the knife from inside my bag, and raise it just as I imagined.

"Wait."

Jacob reaches into his suit jacket and produces a thick

white envelope, its seal misaligned by its bulging contents. I lower the knife and take the envelope from him. Though I don't yet have a solid grasp of how much it should weigh, I slip the envelope into my bag without opening it. I will do that in the car, far away from here, counting the bills under my cell phone's flashlight.

"Ready?" I ask.

This time Jacob gives me space when I raise the knife. I cut open the woman's white dress and use the tip of the blade to sever each crude stitch holding closed the Y-shaped incision that splits her chest. Though heavy, the flaps of skin fold back easily like pages in a well-loved book. Jacob looks on from a few feet back as I spread the already bisected ribcage. He winces, though I don't know if it's from the sight of his beloved cleft before him, or from the cold mineral stench that is rising in front of us. My ears catch the sharp intake of his breath as my hand slides into the woman's chest cavity.

Blood as dark as wet earth oozes over my hands; my fingers puncture a film like the skin on chilled gravy. I think of my brother again, how much warmer he had been—how he still smelled like something that breathes and beats and bleeds—then the look of disappointment that dragged down my mother's face when he failed to rouse at my touch. After that, she chose not to see what I can do; she's never witnessed the sunken faces lifting with joy, the grateful embraces thrown around her only daughter. My mother has never seen the admiration of strangers—more than I ever wanted from her—in that one crystalline moment that I give to them, but couldn't give to her. Hands cupping the young woman's heart, I look over my shoulder at Jacob and attempt a reassuring smile. He smiles back through tears that now flow freely. I gently squeeze the small, firm muscle in my palms. I do it again. I watch the woman's face. I wait for her heart to punch to life in my grip.

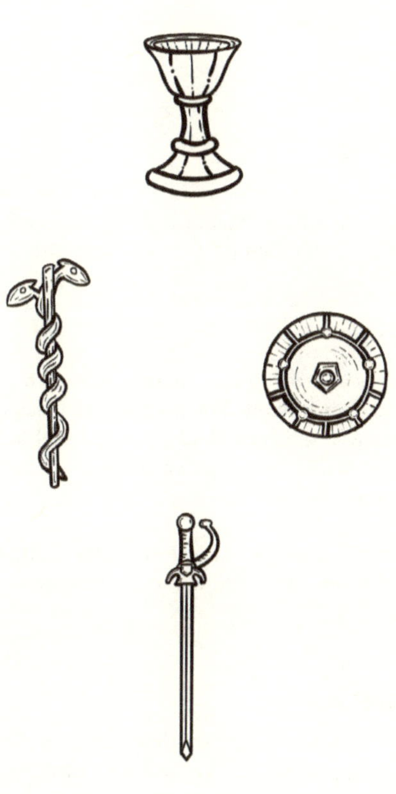

CONTRIBUTORS

Breanna Bright

Breanna Bright is the author of *In The End*. She works as a technical writer in southeast Missouri, and uses her free time travel-ing, reading, and looking for new adventures.

Louis Evans

Louis Evans is a Jewish writer living and working in New York City, on land once inhabited by the Munsee Lenape. It was good land: fertile slash-and-burn fields, fish and shellfish in the river. Lots of beaver, which was popular in Europe . . . you know what happened next.

Louis's work has appeared in *Nature: Futures, Analog SF&F, Interzone,* and more. He's online at evanslouis.com and tweets @ louisevanswrite.

Christopher Hawkins

Christopher Hawkins is an award-winning horror author, with short stories appearing in over a dozen magazine and antholo-gies. He is a former editor of the *One Buck Horror* anthology series, as well as an avid gamer and collector of curiosities. When he's not writing, he spends his time exploring old cemeteries, lurking in museums, and searching for a decent cup of tea.

For free stories and news about upcoming projects, visit his website, www.christopher-hawkins.com, or follow him on X @ chrishawkins.

A. P. Howell

A. P. Howell lives with her spouse, kids, and dog, sometimes near a lake and always near trees. Her stories have appeared in *Daily Science Fiction*, *Little Blue Marble*, and *XVIII: Stories of Mischief & Mayhem*.

She tweets @APHowell and her website is aphowell.com.

Nikoline Kaiser

Nikoline Kaiser is the author of several poems and short stories, including "ode to an asexual" published with *Strange Horizons* and "Last Year's Water" with Pole to Pole Publishing. Her work focuses on family, feminism and queer themes. She lives in Denmark and has a Masters degree in Comparative Literature from Aarhus University.

When not writing, Kaiser works on a project communicating knowledge about women authors around the world and haunts the halls of museums in the hopes of getting to stay among the relics. Visit her at www.nikolinekaiser.wordpress.com.

Jon Lasser

Jon Lasser lives in Seattle, WA with his wife and two children. His stories have appeared in *Galaxy's Edge*, *Little Blue Marble*, *Untethered: A Magic iPhone Anthology*, and elsewhere. He's a graduate of the Clarion West writers workshop.

J. A. W. McCarthy

J.A.W. McCarthy's short fiction has appeared in numerous publications, including *Vastarien, LampLight, Apparition Lit, Tales to Terrify,* and *The Best Horror of the Year Vol 13* (ed. Ellen Datlow). Her debut collection *Sometimes We're Cruel and Other Stories* was published by Cemetery Gates Media. She lives with her husband and assistant cats in the Pacific Northwest, where she gets most of her ideas late at night, while she's trying to sleep.

You can call her Jen on Twitter and Instagram @JAWMcCarthy, and find out more at www.jawmccarthy.com.

Josh Rountree

Josh Rountree writes fantasy, horror, science fiction, and a lot of weird nonsense. His short fiction has appeared in numerous magazines and anthologies, including *Beneath Ceaseless Skies, Realms of Fantasy,* and *A Punk Rock Future.*

A new collection of his short fiction, *Fantastic Americana: Stories,* is available from Fairwood Press.
Josh lives in Texas and tweets about movies, books, and guitars @josh_rountree.

PAMELA COLMAN SMITH

The tarot images in this issue of Arcana are from the deck illustrated by Pamela Colman Smith. It was released in 1909 as the Rider-Waite deck (so named, at that time, in reference to its publisher, William Rider & Son). It remains the most influential and widely used tarot deck. While the impetus for the deck came from Arthur Edward Waite, Colman Smith was responsible for the iconography of the cards.

Pamela Colman Smith also illustrated over twenty books, wrote two collections of Jamaican folklore, edited two magazines, and ran the Green Sheaf Press, a small press devoted to women writers. She continued to write and illustrate throughout her life.

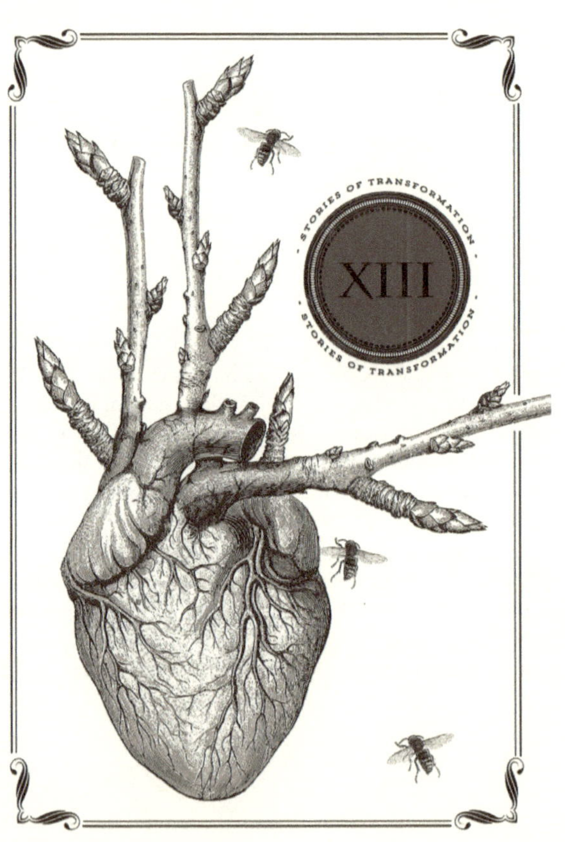
STORIES OF TRANSFORMATION
XIII
STORIES OF TRANSFORMATION

XIII

The thirteenth Tarot card is Death, and he is a symbol not of the end, but of transformation and rebirth. This is the genesis and root of *Thirteen: Stories of Transformation*. The twenty-eight authors of this collection are voices—new and old—who are not afraid to explore what comes next. Whether it be a life after death, a life without love, a life filled with hunger, or the life shared by a ghost. These are stories of the weird, the mythic, the fantastic, the futuristic, the supernatural, and the horrific.

With stories by Liz Argall • M. David Blake • Richard Bowes • George Cotronis • Amanda C. Davis • Julie C. Day • Jetse de Vries • Jennifer Giesbrecht • Daryl Gregory • Rik Hoskin • Rebecca Kuder • Claude Lalumière • Marc Levinthal • Grá Linnaea • Alex Dally MacFarlane • Juli Mallett • Lyn McConchie • Fiona Moore • Gregory L. Norris • Adrienne J. Odasso • Cat Rambo • Andrew Penn Romine • David Tallerman • Tais Teng Richard Thomas • Fran Wilde • A. C. Wise • Christie Yant

Edited by Mark Teppo.

Available at independent bookstores everywhere.

http://www.underlandpress.com

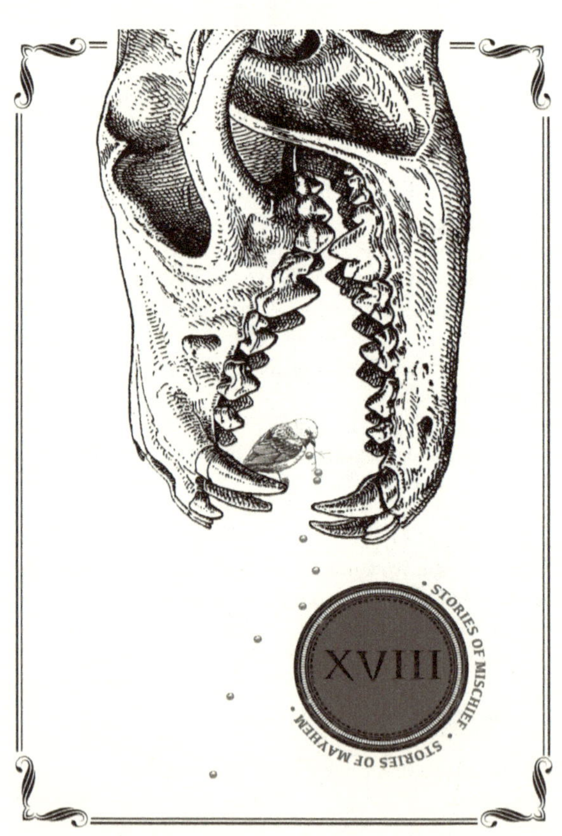

XVIII
STORIES OF MISCHIEF · STORIES OF MAYHEM

XVIII

The eighteenth Tarot card is the Moon, and those who raise their arms to her know she offers Mercy and Severity in equal measure. This is the great river at night, where wolves howl and all doors are open. All futures are possible, and every truth is elusive. This is the source and passion of *Eighteen: Stories of Mischief & Mayhem*. These twenty-four stories from voices—old and new—celebrate the inevitability of fate, the horror of prophecy, and the shivering delight of not knowing what comes next.

Cross over the threshold with us, and explore the strange, the weird, and the fantastic. Do not fear what lies ahead. It is the same as what came before. The only difference is you. This is *Eighteen*, and nothing will be the same.

With stories by Forrest Aguirre • Darin Bradley • Christopher East • Scott Edelman • Nicole Feldringer • Ben Gamblin • Ingrid Garcia • A. P. Howell • Emma Johnson-Rivard • E. E. King • Jessie Kwak • Shannon Lawrence • Gerri Leen • Mark Mills • Christi Nogle Tammie Painter • Josh Rountree • Erica Sage • Lorraine Schein • J. Dee Stanley • Richard Thomas • John Waterfall • Wendy N. Wagner • Todd Zack

Edited by Mark Teppo.

Available at independent bookstores everywhere.

http://www.underlandpress.com